READY
FOR
FABULOUS

Stella wrote the first draft of the Finding Fabulous series
while visiting various places around the world. Although the
books are not autobiographical, she found inspiration in the joy of
unexpected friendships and cultural differences. Stella travels regularly,
always with her laptop, and writes whenever she can. When she's
home, she lives in Gloucestershire. She carries out speaking
engagements about her life as a writer and social entrepreneur.
Ready for Fabulous is her second novel and
the second in the Finding Fabulous series.

Also in the Finding Fabulous series:
How Flora Finds Her Fabulous
Paperback ISBN 978-1-8383109-0-5
Ebook ISBN 978-1-8383109-1-2

Ready for Fabulous
Paperback ISBN 978-1-8383109-2-9
Ebook ISBN 978-1-8383109-3-6

Forever Fabulous (coming soon)

Sign up to receive special offers, bonus content,
book promotions or events and updates from the author

www.stellabookchat.com

If you'd like to connect on social media:
Instagram: StellaBookChat
Twitter: @stellabookchat
Facebook: stellabookchat

READY
FOR
FABULOUS

STELLA STONESTREET

Speedwell

First published in 2021 by Speedwell Publishing
First produced in paperback in 2021

Paperback ISBN 978-1-8383109-2-9
Ebook ISBN 978-1-8383109-3-6

Typeset in Garamond by Jo Guillen Aguilar
Printed in Great Britain by Clays Ltd, Elcograf S.p.A.

As a commitment to a sustainable future this book is
printed on paper made from responsible sources

MIX
Paper from
responsible sources
FSC® C018072

For Cindy
and
feisty ladies everywhere

CHAPTER 1

FLORA

Flora had him in her sights. The only possible beau-to-be in the penny arcade, his flower-power shirt drawing her like a bee to nectar. She had watched him arrive at Seashells Guesthouse, then clocked him in the queue at the fish and chip shop and now, on the pier. His lovely shoulder-length blonde hair flopped over his face as he leaned forward, concentrating on a game of Shindig Pinball.

'I'm Flora, what's your name?'

'Colin.'

'Are you here with your family?'

'Yeah, worse luck.'

'Me too. We're here for the week.'

'Bummer.' He muttered, nudging the machine, still not looking up.

'Yes, it's a bummer,' she said, enjoying the use of the word bummer, despite the fact she'd been crossing the dates off in her diary and had underlined 'Hooray! Holiday Starts Today!' in red pen. 1968 was going to be the year when everything changed for the better. She had been planning her first holiday romance for weeks and according to Cupid's Secret, the most reliable-looking fortune-teller writing machine on the pier, love, luck and marriage were on the cards.

1

'Is this the first time you've been to Weston-super-Mare?' she asked.

'Yeah.'

He wasn't a talker. No matter, she would just have to increase her allure.

'I'm going to be a model. One day soon I'll be on the front cover of Nova.'

With that, he let go of the machine and appraised her. Flora struck a well-rehearsed pose, completed with something between a knowing smile and a pout.

'Farmer's Weekly, more likely.' He smirked and launched another pinball.

'Hey! Don't be like that,' she ventured, but Colin didn't seem to hear and as soon as his game was over, he walked off without a word or a backward glance.

Flora re-examined the little printed card from Cupid's Secret; it said good things were going to happen, but maybe not immediately and definitely not with Colin. She was used to rejection and besides, she still had six more days to find her dream date. She looked around the arcade and settled on a group of boys crowded around the mechanical grabber, trying to win a ten-shilling note, wrapped around a packet of cigarettes. She pictured herself sashaying over, taking the controls and dragging the prize to victory; they'd be so impressed, they'd probably fight over who would be the first to take her dancing. A collective groan told her they had failed and as the group broke up, someone shouted, 'Let's do the dodgems!'. Maybe she could win the prize and take it over to them at the dodgems, or perhaps be more sassy and just go straight there and get in a car next to the dishiest driver? She was still daydreaming of living happily ever after in a country cottage with a dodgem boy when, just like a knight in shining armour, the only man who truly loved her was making his way towards her.

'Ah, there you are, Pickle, how about an ice cream and a bit of fresh air?'

Walking along the promenade on her father's arm was as close as she'd been to any man, but all that was about to change. Sweet sixteen and never been kissed, how she hated that phrase. Never mind that for now; she'd just left school, the world was waiting and she had the assurance of love, luck and marriage in her pocket.

~晚卵~

It soon became apparent why the place was known as Weston-super-Mud: the rest of the holiday had been a washout, horizontal rain lashed across the dismal expanse of grey sand while redundant donkeys sheltered under the pier and seagulls flew inland. Even the arcade lost its appeal and to top it off, the only boy Flora had a decent conversation with was ten-year-old Neville at the guesthouse – a bespectacled little nose-picker who challenged her to a tiddlywinks tournament.

Back home in Coventry, the Summer drizzled on. With nothing more to do than stay indoors and entertain herself, Flora avoided being asked to help with the housework by spending most of the time in her bedroom. She enjoyed re-reading back issues of Jackie magazine; *Twenty Ways to Make New Friends* had some useful tips and *Give Your Looks a Fling!* was most inspiring. If only she had somewhere to go, she could try out Mary Quant's '*lovely pair of shiners*' in the real world, instead of just at home. She applied black mascara, allowing each layer to dry until she had a satisfactory build-up, then carefully drew a line of whitener inside her lower lashes. The best part was swiping on the eyeshadow and hey presto! Twiggy's doe-eyed look. She found a jar of Vaseline in the bathroom cabinet and applied it to her lips for guaranteed kissability. Her campaign to be ready for anything or more specifically, anyone, was right on target.

As part of her reinvention, she refused her mother's offer to run up a new outfit from her collection of Simplicity patterns. The days of looking like a child of the fifties in frocks with over-zealous smocking or ill-fitting slacks were gone. That also went for the mortifying phase of mother-and-daughter outfits, made in the same fabric, Mum's with elaborate frills and buttons, Flora's the plain dumbed-down version. Those dresses were a visual summary of their relationship. Mother first, daughter an afterthought. Or in truth, a mistake. She'd known that from a young age; she was the reason her parents had had to marry and although they seemed to have made the best of it, Flora was all too aware she was an unwelcome guest at a party for two. Well, not for much longer. If everything went to plan, she'd soon meet her Prince Charming and Mum could 'get her life back', whatever that was supposed to be.

At sixteen, she had her own ideas on fashion and asked Dad for a ten-shilling clothing allowance. The hot pants she'd ordered from Freeman's catalogue were a good fit, but the top was a disappointment; if only she had the bazookas. She would have to stop sleeping on her front and do at least twenty press-ups a day if she were ever to be selected by Pan's People. During the bazooka-growing phase, she had better continue to work on her high kick and twirl. She copied the dance moves off Top of the Pops and gave them her own names: the scissor spin and the wiggle jump were surely guaranteed to impress at her interview, so long as she remembered to smile and somehow managed to increase her cup size. Meanwhile, she had a job at Fine Fare, starting Monday.

Although disappointed not to have been accepted at secretarial college, she would be earning her own money and was looking forward to more freedom. After four miserable years at St Margaret's High School for Girls she had only had a handful of so-called friends, other odd-balls forced together by circumstances rather than choice. She hoped a job would also mean meeting a couple of nice girls she could go dancing with at The Regent on a Friday night. If she was ever to get a boyfriend, she would have to go there; everyone knew the slow dance at the end of an evening was the perfect beginning for a dreamy romance.

With just a few days to go before life-changing friendships were formed, she had better rearrange her bedroom; whenever anyone came to visit, she wouldn't want to give the wrong impression. Teddy bears would have to stay in the wardrobe, although still sitting comfortably on the top shelf, and her ballerina jewellery box had better disappear as well. An assortment of Tufty Club posters definitely had to come down but there was no way she would be moving her crushes. Ever since *Dr Zhivago*, she had been mad about Omar Sharif. Slightly stern, brooding and very good looking – what more could anyone want in a man? And if he wasn't too old for Julie Christie, then she was in with a chance; if he were ever to propose, she'd say yes in a jiffy. Next to the love of her life was the second most handsome man in the world, BBC newsreader, Robert Dougall. There was something about his authority while passing on the shocker of the day in a calm, collected manner that made Flora go weak at the knees.

Cliff Richard smiled down from above her bed in his petrol blue velvet suit and fabulously romantic white ruffle. He had earned his place for being such a dish in *Summer Holiday* and for almost winning the Eurovision Song Contest with '*Congratulations*'. She had listened to him continually on the Dansette until her parents agreed she could keep the player in her room if it meant they didn't have to hear 'that blasted song' ever again. Neither of them seemed to like music which sometimes made her wonder if she was adopted.

With roller-skates and a collection of dolls in various stages of undress shoved in a box under her bed, Flora was ready to tackle her bookcase. Barbara Cartland's fragrant reads, arranged alphabetically from *Cupid Rides Pillion*, to *The Viscount's Revenge* filled most of the space while Catherine Cookson's *Fanny McBride* jostled with *The Blind Miller* for space at the end. After an inner debate on how she wanted her new friends to perceive her, Flora decided *Lady Chatterley's Lover* should hide in the wardrobe, on top of a stack of Bunty Annuals.

The top shelf of the bookcase was now free to display her impressive collection of nail polish. They were mostly passed down from Mum, who claimed she had to spend the family allowance on her appearance because having Flora's had ruined her looks. In a circuitous route of just injustice, the resulting overflow of beauty products found its way to the perpetrator. Flora clustered pearly pinks and ravishing reds together in a knowing beautician's display with the most popular colours at the front and the moody purples at the back. She doubted any of her soon-to-be Fine Fare friends would have half the selection and she already knew which colours she would be prepared to give away.

CHAPTER 2

JOHN

John's teenage years had been set up for disappointment while he was still in short trousers. At Elgar Primary School, where post-war bomb damage still pock-marked the playground, his classmates considered him a good enough goalie. Even with his crippled leg, the lack of agility was hardly noticeable in the small space between two dustbins; and the fact he never asked to swap places with the scoring champions made him a popular choice. In the classroom, his ability to respond with witty one-liners increased his popularity and as a star pupil, teachers overlooked his ever-so-slightly arrogant undertone, too keen to chalk up another success on the educational leader board.

When John became the only boy to pass his Eleven Plus, he celebrated by sharing a Gentleman Smoker's Selection Box with a few of his classmates. Huddled in the bike shed, pretend-puffing their way through sickly sweet cigarettes and chewy liquorice pipes, they all agreed the cleverest boy in school would become the next Prime Minister. Another Churchill they cheered, slapping him on the back and passing round the last chocolate cigar for a taste of victory. Little did John realise that his finest hour had already happened and by the end of the Summer holidays, the happiest days of his life would be over.

Upon entering grammar school, where every boy was his academic equal, John discovered the cruel reality of competitive sport. With his leg in a brace, his awkward gait became the brunt of jokes and bullying. Then a few weeks later, the addition of prescription glasses provoked someone to call him *The Limping Spectacle* and before long everyone joined in – even some of the teachers. The fervent teenage fantasy of being attractive enough to get a girlfriend quickly disintegrated to zero, confirmed by the arrival of acne. To be bullied or ignored by the boys was one thing, but knowing that girls giggled and whispered about him in a spiteful way was far worse.

John found sanctuary in the school library. Wedged between a radiator and the lower reaches of the non-fiction department, he left the rocky foothills of social interaction, nasty girls and testosterone-fuelled ballgames, and set off on what would become a lifelong journey of discovery. In awe of the diverse physical, biological and cultural features of the earth's surface, geography became his world.

At university, even with his now unfettered leg, he avoided the dances and social events, telling himself he was above such frivolous pursuits; he was an academic. The closest he'd come to a relationship had been with Margaret Gibson from the Debating Society. She seemed to be attracted to his agile mind and didn't notice his odd gait. There had been a first date at the Lyndon Tea Rooms and then a second at the Open Debate Finals of 1956. Throughout the evening, John had paid her close attention, bought all the drinks and said something nice about her hair. She had even giggled at his joke about subatomic particles. To his dismay, at the end of the evening, she left with the winning first speaker, a philosophy graduate from Trinity. And that was that; his already fragile ego was knocked into full submission.

John's non-existent sex life saw him through university and accompanied him to his first job at Quinton Grammar School where he encouraged bright, jolly boys towards the understanding of katabatic change, and the difference between mesosphere and troposphere. The only female he came in contact with was the elderly school secretary, Miss Timothy, whose sensible haircut and sagging bosoms transmitted a cats and knitting vibe. So, by choice and circumstance, he became a confirmed bachelor and reconciled himself to occasional masturbation into an old sock; a method he'd retained from his youth when fear of Mother's discovery collided with uncontrollable urges. Other than that, he enjoyed a sexless existence in the affable company of tweedy, pipe-smoking colleagues.

In those days, he returned each afternoon to the comfort of number ninety-three Grove Road, where he relayed witticisms and news of the day to Mother over a nice home-cooked evening meal, followed by a good book until cocoa at bedtime. This pleasant routine came to an unexpected end when Quinton Grammar School was relegated to merge with several lesser schools in the district and form a large comprehensive; John, believing this signalled the demise of civilised education, decided to move on.

Much to his astonishment, on arrival at St Margaret's High School for Girls, John appeared to be the subject of speculation. He was one of only three male teachers; the other two conveyed the rudiments of classics and science with eighty-eight years of chalk and talk between them. With just a few tufts of silver hair and dribble-marked ties around their turtle-like necks, they no longer counted as men. So, as the only possible contender for two hundred teenaged girls, Mr Marshall became known as Jonny M, the school crush. His slight disability was inconsequential; he was a male of the species, under retirement age and did at least have two legs in almost working order.

The girls wrote him love notes, sometimes anonymous, other times scribbled in the margins of their homework. Now and then he'd find that a bag of chocolate limes or liquorice comfits had been slipped into his briefcase. Pheromones battled with propriety. Although he hadn't the slightest interest in silly schoolgirl crushes, he felt a certain confirmation that he was not as physically repulsive as he had been led to believe.

Whilst always maintaining a respectable balance between teacher and pupil, John secretly enjoyed the attention. Anyone who knew him well would have noticed an additional spring in his already unusual step. If matters had continued beyond that first autumn term, he may even have developed a bit of swagger, but during a lesson on glacial deposition, while drawing an illustration of arêtes and pyramidal peaks on the blackboard, he was summoned to the headmistresses office to receive an urgent phone call.

The news of his mother's stroke had a devastating effect on John. From then on, outside of teaching the curriculum, he focused his attention on hospital visits, then when there was nothing more they could do, dealt with a series of helpers to nurse her at home. They spent weekends in relative silence, his one-way conversations barely seemed to register, yet still he tried to hang on to what they had enjoyed together. He dug Mother's allotment, tended her dahlias and reported the climatic changes; he heated soup and spoon-fed her supper, then ate alone while she slept.

As the only two of the Marshall family to survive the war, the slow but inevitable separation of their bond was all the more painful. The Coventry Blitz had almost claimed him as well as his father and sister, his tiny toddler leg crushed by falling masonry and the rest of him shielded beneath the kitchen table. Mother and son had clung to each other through the rest of the conflict, first in hospital and later at their new home in Grove Road. John hardly remembered his big sister, Julie, or even his father; nothing remained from his early life, only Mother. And now she was leaving. A steady stream of carers washed and fed her fading body with John in close attendance. When she passed away a few months later, all that remained was her allotment of dahlias and a house full of memories.

CHAPTER 3

FLORA

Flora's father liked to organise their summer holiday well in advance and booked it in January to avoid disappointment. The selection process was a lengthy affair that required spreading an *AA Road Map of Great Britain* over the dining room table, weighted down by *Baedeker's Great Britain*, and *The Motorist's Touring Guide*. With the most favourable route cross-referenced with the latest *Shell Touring Map* for a trustworthy supply of petrol, he would draw up a shortlist. In terms of destination, the one thing they all agreed upon was that a holiday wasn't a holiday unless it was beside the sea; other than that, the three of them were on different pages of the guidebook.

No matter where they went, Flora knew a week away would be prefixed by several hours of torture in Dad's pride and joy, a two-door Triumph Herald. Dad in his driving gloves, giving a running commentary on how well 'She' was handling the road, Mum next to him, silent and chain-smoking before they'd even left Coventry. As for Flora, she hunkered down in the back, sucking her way through a tin of powder-coated travel sweets to fend off the threat of nausea and boredom.

Being a 'car man' meant Dad added five or ten-minute conversational delays at any given opportunity; petrol stations, beauty spots or any place where men gathered together while women spent a penny, packed up a picnic or simply sat in the car, waiting. Flora knew that every pencilled cross on Dad's road map marked the spot where two or three men would walk around the car slowly, kicking a tyre here and there, drawing on their cigarettes in contemplation while Dad trotted out a string of sickening compliments. Like schoolboys admiring a prized conker, according to Mum.

'Look at her: honest, reliable and beautiful, just like the perfect woman.' Flora knew he was only half-joking. 'She'll go from nought to sixty in twenty-eight point nine seconds, smooth as you like.' Given the chance, he'd go one step further, stroke the bonnet and say, 'She's a beautiful ride.' For some reason, this comment drove Mum mad and provided Flora with the rare occasion when they could exchange an eye-rolling tut-and-sigh combo.

According to Dad, half the pleasure of an annual holiday was the journey, which meant the further away, the better. In this respect, Coventry was the perfect starting point, being as far from the sea as geographically possible. Eastbourne, Tenby, Broadstairs and Penzance had been ticked off the list in recent years. Last year, he had chosen Weston-super-Mare, the closest to home. For any normal person it would have been little more than a three-hour drive, but Dad had gone the long way round in order to take 'Her' over a new feat of engineering called the Severn Bridge.

As it turned out, Weston-super-Mare had been one of Dad's better choices, at least there had been a decent pier and an arcade, and although Flora's holiday romance hadn't materialised, she was ever the optimist. Perhaps Summer Holiday, 1969 was going to be even better. Wherever Dad decided on this year, hopefully there would be a funfair or a penny arcade and maybe even a dancehall. Perhaps she could befriend a girl of her own age and they could go dancing together and meet some boys.

Or perhaps not.

'It says here, "a famous resident played, *Nearer, My God, to Thee* to calm the passengers while the Titanic sank in 1912". How about that?'

'That's just another reason why we shouldn't go all the way to bloody Bridlington –'

'Honestly, Flora do you have to use such language? Ever since Fine Fare you're a changed girl, and not for the better I might add.'

'Blackpool's much better; it's got everything.'

'Blackpool? No, absolutely not. I'd rather we didn't go at all than go to a place like that. No, Bridlington is just the ticket. Bracing coastal walks, a nice little harbour and an excellent choice of scenic excursions for your mother.'

'What about what I want? I'm going to be bored stiff, as usual.'

'Mrs Fraser's chilblains are playing havoc, you should see them. Fingers like sausages,' said Mum, who had just come in from talking over the fence to next door. 'What's that, Flora?'

'I said I'll be bored stiff on holiday if we have to go to Bridlington.'

'Bridlington?' She leaned over Dad's shoulder and scanned the guidebook. 'It looks very nice. Just the ticket.'

'Can't we go to Blackpool for a change? Somewhere more happening?'

'Happening? Whatever that's supposed to mean, the answer's no. We'll go wherever your father says. He works hard all year, he deserves to go wherever he chooses.'

'Well, I work too.'

'Is that what you call putting a few tins on a shelf? Really, Flora, you have no idea what real work is.'

'Hey! I work full time in a proper job and get paid a wage for it.'

'And ever since you were born, I've worked far harder. My day doesn't end at five o'clock, I don't get days off and I don't get paid. How about that?'

'How about what?' Flora knew this was only leading one way, it always did.

'Don't you speak to me like that young lady. You should be grateful for everything you have. The sacrifices I've had to make. I could have been someone, if it weren't for you.'

Flora could recite the rest of the script by heart. Over the last couple of years, Mum's sacrifices were brought to her attention on a regular basis while Dad sat by without saying a word. There had been a time when he'd intervened and things would calm down, but lately they seemed to close ranks.

'Your mother has a point, Flora, you're old enough to give her a hand around the house.'

'But I'm working.'

'You don't contribute financially. It's not that we need the money, but perhaps it would teach you a few values.'

'So, you want to take my wages off me now? It's not fair, you just make all the rules.'

'Yes, and that's just how it should be.' Her mother was opening her handbag; the next thing she'd say was, she was at the end of her tether. Then she would light a cigarette and stop speaking to anyone for ages so Dad was forced to battle on alone.

'Now go to your room and let Mum and I organise our summer holiday in peace. And don't look at me like that, Flora, it's time you appreciated your mother more. Showed some respect.'

'Well, she doesn't respect me, so –'

'Go to your room!'

~✺~

The supposed four-hour journey to Bridlington turned into an inevitable six and a half, with stops to picnic in a light rain, fill up with petrol, admire the view and at four o'clock, have a flask of tea with a slice of Mum's holiday cake. The holiday cake tradition had started years before, whereby a baked treat in a tin would be unveiled. Mum's little moment. Flora already knew it was chocolate but pretended to be surprised just to keep the peace. It was bad enough being stuck in the back of a car, without being shouted at by both parents from the front seats.

Bridlington turned out to be almost as boring as Flora had imagined: full of old people and no dancing, not even a proper arcade and absolutely no chance of making friends, let alone find a potential romance. A small ray of hope presented itself on the third day when the landlady asked if she would like to take part in Bridlington's annual carnival.

'The Seafood Chippy's one mermaid short of a fish supper,' she declared. If Flora wouldn't mind it would save the day because Wendy had one of her heads and Norma was already committed.

'Mermaid, eh? Go on, Flora, you might enjoy it,' said Dad.

'And you didn't want to do the coastal walk in any case,' added Mum.

Flora had noticed recently that her parents were always trying to get rid of her, but dressing up as a gorgeous mermaid and be paraded through the town on a low loading trailer sounded quite glamorous; it might be fun to be on show. Good practice for when she became a professional dancer.

'That's settled then, I'll take you over to the chippy after breakfast so you can try out the costume,' said the landlady, already rushing away to clear plates on another table.

Flora daydreamed her way through eggs, bacon and three slices of toast. Instead of trailing behind Mum and Dad on some boring cliff-top walk, her day was now full of endless possibilities. Starting with two strategically placed scollop shells and a silver-sequinned fish-tail skirt and ending with Bridlington Summer Carnival's beautiful mystery mermaid making the front page of the Evening Gazette; a humble beginning leading to who knows where? A dazzling career in

15

the public eye. Television. Possibly world fame. Then she'd have her pick of boyfriends.

Seafood Chippy was only a few streets away. Flora could have gone on her own, but the landlady seemed keen to accompany her, explaining that the owners were 'Proper Yorkshire', whatever that meant. She explained they were keen to win the Best Carnival Float because it would get them free publicity and a chance to invite the Mayor and his entourage to partake in their fish supper instead of going to The Town Fryer on the other side of the harbour.

'Here's she is.' The landlady spoke over the clang of the bell above the door and ushered Flora in. A woman was mopping the floor with Jeyes Fluid while her husband gutted mackerel on the countertop. A combined heady aroma of chemicals and fish assaulted Flora's nostrils while a discussion was taking place in accents she barely understood.

'She's a weighty lass,'

'Wee Wendy 'ood av bin betta.'

'Aye, 'appen that.'

'Is un in t'puddin' club?'

'Preggers? You're not, are you love?' The landlady gave Flora a steely glance and a moment of time froze while her gaze dropped down to scrutinise her midriff. Without another word, she then propelled Flora towards the back of the shop and through a curtain of coloured plastic strips, saying, 'Come on, Marge, get the costume sorted. If you have to let it out a stretch, so be it.'

As Marge propped her mop against the wall and wiped her hands on her apron, the landlady was already leaving the shop and was gone with another double clang of the bell before Flora could say she'd changed her mind.

It only took one look at the mermaid's costume to know she would never be Bridlington's darling. Following an almost incomprehensible conversation between the Seafood Chippy proprietors, Flora surmised that as there was a shortage of volunteers, they would have to reshuffle the cast. Even the role of jolly fisherman, with his red cheeks and yellow sou'wester would have been preferable to becoming a portion of battered cod, but there was no point in arguing. With all the kerfuffle, trying to make the mermaid costume fit, there was no time to waste and Flora soon found herself squeezed into an orange cardboard 'crispy batter' coating, with her hands and face slathered in greasepaint to match.

Grateful that her parents had opted to miss the carnival and stick to the plan of an all-day walk along the coast to Flamborough Head, Flora was at least spared the humiliation of Dad taking a snap for the family album.

By the time her parents returned to the guesthouse, Flora had scrubbed at her hands and face enough to reduce the residual orange tinge to what she hoped looked more like a suntan.

'Well, you missed a treat,' said Dad, looking windswept and happy. 'We saw auks, gannets and herring gulls, didn't we, love?'

'Oh and darling little puffins. And those kitty things.'

'Kittiwakes.'

It was only after they'd counted all the seabirds off their fingers and retold the sighting of a grey seal or maybe a porpoise that they asked how her day at the carnival had gone.

'Fine.'

'That's good,' said her mother, 'I'm ravenous after all that walking. What was it twelve miles? Thirteen? So, what's on the menu this evening I wonder?'

Flora didn't care, so long as it wasn't fish and chips.

~ⁿᵈᵍ~

After a long week of nothing much else and what seemed like an even longer drive home, Flora was back at work. No one asked her where she'd been, but if they had, her reply would have been *Boring Bridlington*. For once she was glad for the lack of interest. The sooner the whole episode was forgotten, the better.

The highlight of Flora's Summer was a small promotion at Fine Fare. There was no extra pay but instead of just restocking the shelves, she was now in charge of displaying special offers and new produce in a way that customers might make a spontaneous purchase. As most housewives bought the same things every week, it was a challenge to provoke a moment of madness when a family-sized packet of Gypsy Creams might take president over the usual Rich Tea; Flora's suggestion to rearrange the window displays more regularly and pin up a hand-written poster paid off too. Sales were slightly up throughout the autumn, into winter.

It wasn't the romantic interlude she'd been hoping for, but the small increase in responsibility and the few words of praise from her manager turned out to be the best thing that happened in 1969.

Soon after the New Year, seeing Dad back at the dining room table with his road map and guidebooks, Flora had all but given up on the idea of a holiday romance; his dismal choice was bound to be another letdown. Life was a letdown. She'd be eighteen this summer, plenty old enough to move to a more happening place on her own. Perhaps she should join a band, become a singer? Or maybe now was the time to contact Pan's People? She'd never find fame, living in the suburbs of Coventry. She couldn't even find a boyfriend.

CHAPTER 4

JOHN

Until the Summer of 1970, John's harem of dahlias was his only concession to love. 'The Girls', nurtured into annual splendour at his late mother's allotment, were apron strings from beyond the grave. The attention he lavished on Nancy Ellen, Sorrento Girl and Taratahi Ruby, was rewarded with a delight of waterlily and collarette hot pinks, reds and zesty citrus; a reciprocal relationship with no need for fuss or small talk.

So, when the seeds of courtship were sown in the dry goods section of Fine Fare, it was without John's intention or desire. There were no cupid's arrows or any such nonsense, just a shop assistant stacking the 'deal of the week' into a bargain-sized pyramid.

'Excuse me, miss.' His hand almost touched hers as he stretched for the upper reaches of Lipton flo-thru teabags.

'One or two?' asked the girl, passing him a box from her trolley. There was something familiar about her freckled face.

'Didn't you used to go to St Margaret's?'

She looked at him, her mouth slightly open; he caught a glimpse of pink bubble gum stuck on her bottom teeth.

'Mr Marshall! Fancy seeing you in a place like this.'

'Is it Frances Jones?'

'No, I'm Flora Jones, you used to teach me geography.'

'Indeed.' He tried to think what else he could say. Why on earth had he started a conversation? 'Have you worked here for long?'

'About two years, it's better than the carpet factory, except I don't always get Saturdays off, but it's two and six more in wages.'

'I see.' It was always awkward meeting past pupils. A teacher's relationship doesn't transition with ease from absolute authority to, well, nothing much at all.

'How about you, Mr Marshall, are you still teaching geography at St Margaret's?' She continued to stack boxes of tea, although much slower than before.

'Well, yes. I expect I'll be there until I retire,' he said, and quickly added, 'which is several decades from now.' Did that make him sound younger or older? He didn't know.

'Do you live locally? I haven't seen you in here before.'

'No, I was just passing. I spotted the special offer in the window.' He detected the faint scent of something familiar. Yardley English Rose?

'Everyone likes a bargain, Mr Marshall,' said Flora with a wink.

She was almost pretty when she smiled.

'Please, call me John,' he said.

'Alright, John it is, though we used to call you Jonny M at school, did you know that?'

'Yes, thank you. I am quite aware of all the staff's nicknames.'

Flora's trolley was now empty. 'Well, it's lovely to see you, call in again. I'm always here.' She shot him another smile and wheeled back to the stockroom.

~~~

Up to the day John popped into Fine Fare, life as a bachelor had spread before him like the Kalahari Desert; at the age of thirty-three, he had no social life. Besides teaching, the world of social interaction was a barren land only interrupted by the occasional mildly irritating feature – a dentist appointment or an after school event. Monday to Friday provided a simple routine of geography lessons, where almost all communication was channelled through the blackboard, and a cryptic crossword as a diversion from pointless staffroom chitter-chatter at lunchtime. After school, a stack of marking kept him company up until the evening news on the wireless, after which he prepared an evening meal of either salad and cold meat or tinned stew, depending on the weather, followed by a few hours with his library books.

Sometimes, he played Mother's record collection – Frank Sinatra, Nat King Cole, Perry Como and all the greats, or he watched *Horizon, World in Action* or *Wicker's World* on the black and white television set he had hired from Radio Rentals the previous year. Originally he had only splashed out to watch the all-night broadcast of Apollo 11 landing on the moon, but he'd kept it on.

Mother had wanted him to marry. In a way, it was her dying wish; even though she could no longer speak, it was an unanswered request she'd hinted at for years. He knew he'd let her down in that department, but there was no need for another person in his life, no need at all. On Saturday there was always a much-anticipated trip to the library, followed by a cheese sandwich for lunch and an afternoon at the allotment. Then a whole glorious Sunday to read, undisturbed. With two intermissions for food: a lunchtime grilled lamb cutlet with tinned peaches for afters, and later, a high tea treat of sardines on toast, a couple of fig rolls and a slice of fruit loaf. Throughout the day the teapot was replenished in between chapters.

The school holidays were a blissful oasis of Sunday-like days, uninterrupted by anyone apart from Mrs Higgs, the cleaner, who had been dusting, washing and ironing at number ninety-three for as long as John could remember. Keeping Mrs Higgs on sustained the living memory of Mother with a heady olfactory cocktail of Mansion Polish, carbolic soap and Brasso.

This pleasure was sometimes supplemented by her provision of an ovenproof dish containing a Lancashire hotpot or a rhubarb crumble with instructions for reheating, written in the old lady's rheumatic hand. '*Heet ovin 350. Middel shelf 25 min*'. John fought a desire to take out his red pen but Mrs Higgs' excellent home cooking was reason enough to forgive a poor education. That withstanding, there was still no need to interact with her. During the school holidays he escaped to the library or the allotment before she arrived, thus avoiding pointless conversation about the weather, the state of the country or the shortcomings of the impending decimalisation. An occasional note and the agreed ten shillings placed on the kitchen table sufficed.

Once a month he enjoyed the added pleasure of a fresh-off-the-press issue of National Geographic. He justified the extravagance of an annual subscription by considering it a Christmas present to himself since there was no one else to buy for. Whichever day of the week the magazine flumped onto the doormat, he displayed it on the coffee table still in its wrapper until Sunday, by which time the anticipation of opening it was at a peak.

On one such Sunday in June, after a hurried bowl of cornflakes and a quick wash-up and tidy away, John laid a tray with a cup and saucer, made a fresh pot of tea and carried it through to the sitting room. He ceremoniously poured himself a cup of tea, then settled down to open the familiar package. While he sat with the mint copy of National Geographic across his knees, inhaling the inky pages, and perusing the index, he struggled to concentrate. Then, on beginning what promised to be an excellent four-page feature on volcanic activity, he had to reread a paragraph on phreatomagmatic clasts twice before giving in to an unexpected intrusion in the form of a daydream.

Flora Jones in her Fine Fare overalls. The neatly stacked shelves, and evenly spaced rows. Her deft handling of the pricing gun as she marked goods down to half price. Each label, squarely placed in the same position. Bang. Bang. Bang. The vivid mental depiction was most unnerving, but he couldn't control his imagination. As she handed him an economy-sized box of broken biscuits while blowing an impressive sphere of pink bubblegum, his dormant libido was aroused from near extinction to the threat of a Strombolian-like eruption.

The next day, John found himself to be 'just passing' Fine Fare and felt compelled to pop in. Flora was almost in the same spot as last time, again, restocking the shelves from an overloaded trolley. He had no intention of ever eating a Vesta Beef Curry, but he bought one in any case. Thereafter, he detoured down the aisles of convenience two or three times a week on his way home from St Margaret's. As Flora was a shelf-stacker, it followed that he would have to buy whatever she was restocking. If only she worked on the tills, he could get away with a necessary purchase of scouring pads or potatoes. Instead, he had accumulated a kitchen cupboard full of Farley's Rusks, Piccalilli and Angel Delight. With such unnecessary expenditure and all for hardly more than a quick, 'Hello, how are you?', he took the plunge and suggested a stroll in the park after work.

The first walk was no more than a circuitous route around the flowerbeds towards the bus stop, with a stilted conversation about the weather, and the possibility of 1970 having a disappointing summer after such a heavy snowfall in March. John was about to say he hoped it would rain at least twice a week from thereon to water his dahlias when Flora mentioned an impending family holiday to Llandudno.

'Two years ago we went to Weston-super-*Mud*, then *Boring* Bridlington but this year we're going to Wales, which is almost abroad. I'm really looking forward to it, except Dad wants us to climb Snowdon. He's such a square.' She was chewing pink gum again and blew a nonchalant bubble.

'Well, I hope you pack a raincoat; given Wales's topographical inclines and exposure to the prevailing south-westerly winds. I think you'll find the eastern flank of Snowdon is one of the wettest places in Britain.' Pleased with his off-the-cuff geography lesson, it took him a moment to notice Flora's frown, then quickly added, 'However, Llandudno is in what we call a "rain shadow", so you can expect less than thirty inches per annum.'

'I'll be sure to tell Dad,' was all Flora said.

John stood next to her at the bus stop, feeling awkward. She'd been so chatty before, he hadn't needed to think of something to say. When nothing came to mind, he almost gave an audible sigh when her number twenty-two swung into view.

'So, same time on Thursday?' he called after her.

As the bus disappeared around the corner, he turned to walk a few stops further on to save the fare and to contemplate his feelings. Flora was a very pleasant girl, despite being of average intelligence. She had a nice homely way about her and that made him feel comfortable. Perhaps next time instead of walking to the bus stop, which had taken less than fifteen minutes, he should suggest a sit down somewhere; a flask of tea might be a welcome diversion, something to add value to what he inwardly referred to as their 'liaison'.

By the following week, the 'walks' included sitting on John's travel rug in the late afternoon sun, with a flask of tea and a few Rich Tea biscuits he'd bought from home, wrapped in a clean handkerchief. Twice, Flora mentioned a nearby cafe that served peach melbas with squirty cream and extra sauce. But if they went there, he would have to buy one for himself as well, when he could just open a tin of peaches at home.

'I find it really rather refreshing to sit outdoors with a nice cup of tea, don't you?' he insisted. At the same time, he wondered if Flora could taste the slightly odd flavour imparted by the ageing thermos flask. No matter, he would persist with the tea and perhaps he could bring a couple of boiled egg sandwiches as a treat.

CHAPTER 5

FLORA

A week in Wales was enough to convince Flora she wanted to travel. Seeing the unpronounceable place names and listening to the locals speaking Welsh was thrilling. If only she could replace the endless grey skies and mournful horizon with tropical scenery, and the screeching gulls with flamingoes, she would have been in paradise.

'*Bore da.*' The smiling landlady, Mrs Owens, spoke in a soft lilting tone. 'Eggs, laverbread and a nice cup of tea, is it?'

The food was awful, but Flora reasoned they couldn't grow mangoes or pineapples in Llandudno. She would have to persuade Dad to let them go properly abroad next year. Maybe Spain. She would have a whole year to learn to play the castanets like the young heroine in '*The Flamenco Gypsy Princess*', and maybe she could have dancing lessons too. Did they do the cha-cha as well, or just the flamenco? She'd learn whichever one had the best costume and maybe try and learn a few useful words and phrases. Although she was still trying to get to grips with Mrs Owens and her 'bore da', so maybe languages weren't her forte.

Flora loved the cosy guest house, sitting in a bay window seat with a bodice-ripper romance and a view of the sea. She would much rather stay there than get up at the crack of dawn to spend the day conquering Mount Snowdon with Mum and Dad. Clutching her abdomen and pretending to have her monthlies had always got her off games at school. With hardly a need for theatricals, let alone the backup plan of making herself sick, it was quickly agreed she was in no fit state to attempt the summit. With scarcely more than a brief discussion, she was left with five shillings and the whole day to herself.

After a solitary breakfast in the guesthouse, she wandered along the seafront. Dodging a rush of squealing children with buckets and spades at the ready, while parents unloaded cars full of grandparents and picnics, she realised how similar her Summer holidays had always been. As an only child, they were almost more lonely than being at home. It was two years since a holiday romance in Weston-super-Mare had failed to materialise, and she preferred not to remember Bridlington, but now she was more mature, she knew that wasn't how it worked. She had read a motto somewhere: *It's hard to find the path of love, when your heart is full of hope. It's even harder to find a towel when your eyes are full of soap.* Well, she couldn't help hoping. At almost eighteen years of age, she really should have a boyfriend soon.

Perhaps she should try and lose weight? At school she'd been quite a bit chubbier than the other girls, and when Dad started saying things like, 'Who's my little Plumpy?' she'd had to ask him to stop. He changed it to Pickle which still somehow made her feel bad; she would have preferred Princess or Treasure. She couldn't start a diet on holiday, especially when there was real Italian ice cream on offer. Next week she'd start a new regime and tell Mum it was salads and fresh fruit from then on.

She was approaching a parade of shops selling fishing nets and souvenirs. She would look for something with Welsh written on it; the more foreign, the better. While she was at it she'd better choose something for John, he probably wouldn't appreciate an ashtray or a miniature Welsh dragon, but he'd scribbled his address on a spare page in his pocket diary and ripped it out saying, 'Just in case you feel inclined to send a postcard.'

Flora glanced over the garish selection of saucy seaside cartoons: *I mean to stick it out for another week*, declared a fat-bottomed woman in her enormous red and white striped swimsuit. Another large lady seated next to her diminutive husband claimed, *He's enjoying the shade!* Bottoms were pinched, someone had lost little Willy and a statuesque barmaid offered a pie and a pint with a wink. The other cards are dull by comparison; The Great Orme tramway, the West Shore at sunset and then, there it was, the perfect card for John; Snowdonia half-shrouded in mist. She liked the little girls in Welsh national costume with '*Croeso i Gymru – Welcome to Wales*' emblazoned beneath their feet. Why not buy both? It was a shame she didn't have Ava Schulze and Mary O'Connor's address but they'd never been proper school friends; she'd never even been to their houses for tea.

She bought the cards, a stick of pink Llandudno rock and a *Cymru am Byth* keyring, then planned how to fill the rest of the day. If she had an Orange Maid and sat on the beach for a bit, then maybe watched the Punch and Judy show, she could wander back to the guesthouse in time for lunch. Later, she'd write her cards and go to the post office on her way to the pier for a proper sit-down ice cream sundae in Bertorelli's Ice Cream Emporium. After that, she'd have a go on the Penny Falls and have some candy floss to keep herself going until supper time. Mum and Dad hadn't said what time they'd be back, supposedly not until late. If they weren't back by six, she would have fish and chips and a bottle of Dandelion and Burdock on the beach.

Back at the guesthouse, the dining room was full of waiting guests and no sign of any lunch. Flora, knocked on the kitchen door and popped her head in.

'Are you alright, Mrs Owens?'

The usually cheerful landlady was throwing lettuce onto plates and didn't look up when she said, 'I've only just got back from the hospital, my Gaynor's gone into labour, see.'

'Can I help? I could cut those tomatoes if you like?' Flora avoided helping in the kitchen at home, not because she didn't want to, but because experience told her she and her mother couldn't be alone in the confines of a small space without a falling out.

'Oh, would you? Gaynor's gone breech and I've only myself. It's a fine to-do.'

Flora added wedges of tomato and slices of ham to twenty-three willow-patterned plates and went out to the dining room. She retrieved them from the serving hatch and delivered them to the waiting guests with an apology here and a cheerful comment there, enjoying the interaction with the families as they tucked in.

'Well, you are a good girl,' said the landlady, passing the last plates through to her. 'It's a blessing you're here; I was off my feet.'

With a further twenty-three slices of arctic roll cut, served and eaten, Mrs Owens cleared and tidied the dining room while Flora washed up. If she had her own kitchen, she would enjoy preparing meals, so she could have dinner parties and experiment with foreign ingredients. Fine Fare had recently started a foreign food shelf: dried spaghetti, Vesta Beef Curry and a curiously named Tikka Masala paste – she had never had to restock that because nobody seemed to buy it.

'Here we are, love. What with Gaynor and everything, well, I couldn't have managed without you. Come, sit by here.' Mrs Owens had hastily made their lunch with the remainder of ingredients and added an extra slice of ham to their plates.

'Thanks,' said Flora, dolloping salad cream over her lettuce. 'I think I'd like to be a cook, I did home economics at school.'

'Well, why not? And you'd make a lovely little wife for someone. Courting, are you?'

'Not exactly,' She meant to say 'no', but 'not exactly' sounded better than almost-eighteen-and-never-been-kissed. Mrs Owens was giving her a quizzical look. 'Well, not officially, but I have sort of been seeing someone.'

'Oh, married is he?'

'No!'

'Well, what's the big secret then?'

'It's not a secret, it's just that he's never asked if I'd go on a date. He just meets me after work and we go for a walk, have a cup of tea. That sort of thing.'

'Well, that sounds a lot like courting to me. Maybe he's shy. My Trevor, God rest his soul, he was awful shy, used to stand under a tree opposite my house for hours. Rain or shine. My mother asked him in for a cuppa in the end. Silly bugger! We were married twenty-three years. Dead now. Cancer.'

'Oh.' Flora gave the happy-sad story a moment of respect. During the silence she thought of John. At first, he hadn't been more than just someone she knew, but now she thought about it, he was also a quite handsome, sometimes funny man she liked. And older, with a sort of tummy tingling air of authority. 'So, you think John and I are, um, courting?'

'Of course you are. There's only one reason why grown men go for walks in the park and that's to do with the birds and the bees.'

The conversation with Mrs Owens had been a revelation; John was friendly and why else would he meet her from work if he wasn't a suitor? And yes, he was quite dishy. Just thinking about him made her tummy feel fizzy all over again. If he felt the same way about her, then they were a match made in heaven. Flora offered to help Mrs Owens prepare the evening meal, she wanted to hear more about her take on 'the birds and the bees'. It would be better than eating alone in any case but with only two hours spare, there wouldn't be time to write John's cards, go to the post office and the pier. She definitely deserved a treat from Bertorelli's Ice Cream Emporium before peeling a pile of vegetables. The postcards would have to wait.

～⁂～

The last few days of the holiday seemed to fly by. In between an excursion to Rhyl and another to Conwy Castle, Flora helped Mrs Owens in the kitchen and on the last day was rewarded with ten shillings and a visit to see Gaynor's baby in hospital.

'I don't know if the baby's early or if Gaynor's muddled up on dates,' said Mrs Owens. 'Come to think of it, she seemed to find a husband in a hurry, if you know what I mean. Barry Jones took her on, but he's not up to much.'

'In a hurry?'

'I don't know what goes on back in England, but if you live here, being up the pole without a husband is suicide.'

'Oh, right.' Flora had heard about unmarried mothers, the shame, the forced adoptions. She'd never let that happen to her. She'd rather die than give away her baby. Then again, seeing Gaynor's screeching little creature hadn't filled her with maternal emotions either.

'I wonder if that little scrap isn't something to do with Dai Probert. She's got his hair and an awful lot of it for a month premature. Two weeks late, more like.' Mrs Owens didn't seem at all concerned about who the father was. Flora doubted her mother would be so accommodating. The only good thing about not having a proper boyfriend was that she'd never get pregnant. Almost-eighteen-and-never-been-kissed.

While Dad carried suitcases to the car and Mum went to buy some Welsh Cakes, Flora ran to the post office and while standing in the queue, quickly wrote John's postcards. She'd planned to be creative, poetic even, but in the end she dashed off a quick, 'Wish you were here', on the first card and signed off with a sophisticated, 'Yours sincerely, Flora J'. As she was next to be served at the counter, the second card had to be written under pressure. A girl at St Margaret's had had a letter from her pen friend with S.W.A.L.K on the back of the envelope. That would have to do.

CHAPTER 6
JOHN

While Flora was in Llandudno, John had plenty of time to think about the new avenue of social interaction she had provided. Two or three times a week he had found himself arriving outside Fine Fare just before closing time. He then enjoyed an hour or so, regaling Flora with stories of his university days, past triumphs of the debating society and the time he visited Hadrian's Wall. All in all, she offered a new and appealing structure to his routine. Now, in her absence, his days felt somewhat loose and baggy. He hadn't expected to miss the conversations or the sense of purpose.

What if it came to a permanent end? He was still waiting for a postcard and it was already Thursday; did that mean she'd forgotten him? What if she refused his next offer of tea and an egg sandwich? And what about his future? The chances of meeting another Flora were slim indeed, given that she was the first person to share his picnic blanket since his and Mother's day trip to Kenilworth for The National Dahlia Society's Annual Show in 1962.

Until Mother became ill, he'd never thought about the future being any different. Then with her passing he had been so stricken with grief, he had retreated into the safety of books and isolation. But now that he had met Flora, he was surprised to discover human interaction in limited amounts to be a pleasant diversion. And looking ahead, there may be times when having another person around the house would be rather useful. Mrs Higgs had always been there to pop in when he was under the weather and fuss over him with offers of a hot toddy or an extra blanket, but she was already past retirement age. He would soon be charged with the task of finding another cleaner in any case. Flora was pleasant, young, healthy. Was she too young? No. A fifteen-year age-gap wasn't unheard of. And she seemed to like him; long may that last. He had better make sure of it.

~~~

On Flora's eighteenth birthday, John stood in front of the bathroom mirror and thumbed his nose upwards while tilting his head this way and that. He clipped at a few stray nasal hairs and then scrutinised his reflection for further remedial work. He re-did his well-worn side-parting with the tortoiseshell comb he had taken to carrying in his jacket pocket, smoothed down any wayward hairs and polished his glasses. To add a little magnetism, he would take Mother's advice, 'Women go weak at the knees after a whiff of Old Spice.' She had given him the bottle in 1963, as one of her pretexts to saying he should think about finding someone to give her some grandchildren. Seven years later, it was still unused at the back of the bathroom cabinet. He took the lid off, sniffed and recoiled. Crikey! Women were a mystery at times. No matter, he had to throw everything at the situation, even if it meant smelling like a condiment. Tonight was the night.

Liberally doused in very old, Old Spice, John waited for Flora outside Berni Inn feeling agitated and half hoping she wouldn't turn up. He would give her ten minutes after the agreed time, in case she was running late. Of codurse she was going to turn up; she'd been as friendly as ever on her return from holiday and when those postcards had finally arrived, she'd written S.W.A.L.K on one of them. His research revealed, much to his surprise and delight, that it stood for sealed-with-a-loving-kiss. Surely that was testament enough?

His gurgling intestines contracted when the familiar sight of his intended came into view and he stepped forwards to meet her. With an awkward peck on the cheek, he whisked her inside for a two-course steak dinner; the fact it was on offer at a special promotional price of ten and six was, fortuitous.

'Now then, what'll you have to drink, Flora? There's orange squash, or maybe one of those Coca-colas?' The prices were quite reasonable, considering.

'I'd like a Babycham, please. It is my eighteenth, after all,' came the reply.

He had been so wound up about the evening's agenda, he'd almost forgotten he had invited her out for dinner in lieu of a birthday present. A double whammy of both a celebration and a present, he'd said.

'Ah yes, of course, Babycham.' Hopefully, she wouldn't want another at one shilling and six a pop. Still, it was a worthy investment.

Flora chatted excitedly about the transistor radio her parents had given her as a birthday present and the fact she was going to start having driving lessons in the next few weeks. John ate his steak without particular enjoyment and then hurried through his Black Forest gateau, too nervous to notice it was still slightly frozen in the middle.

Now was the moment.

He was feeling hot and fiddled with his collar. Hopefully, his glasses wouldn't steam up.

'Flora?'

Flora had picked up her Knickerbocker Glory glass to tip the remains into her open mouth.

'Eh?' Her tongue was out, ready to catch the strawberry as it gathered speed.

'I've something important to ask you.' He had already considered getting down on one knee but worried about his dodgy leg. The moment would lose all reverence if she had to help him up again. Instead, he moved his chair closer to hers and waited.

'Mmm,' she patted her midriff.

'Flora, my love, I was wondering if –'

'That was the bees-knees.' Flora had a small cluster of hundreds-and-thousands in the corner of her mouth. John thought about dabbing them off with his paper napkin, but took the plunge and reached for her hand instead.

'Flora, would you do me the great honour of becoming my wife?' It was a line he'd practised many times over the past two weeks, and now it was out.

'Oh!'

John's Black Forest was spinning at full velocity in his digestive tract and competed with a rapidly increasing heartbeat into a crescendo of anxiety. He waited for her reply. He hadn't considered anything but an instant, 'Yes'; had he misread the signs? Was it the age gap? He stumbled on, 'It's just that you would make me the happiest man alive.' And to give it a youthful twist he added, 'We're a team, you and me,' inwardly cringing at the grammar. 'So, what do you say?'

'Yes' said Flora.

'Yes?'

'Yespialadocious!'

Forgiving both their misuses of the English language, he grappled inside his jacket pocket and pulled out a folded hankie. With shaky hands, he unwrapped his late mother's diamond ring. She'd been wearing it when she died and it had travelled on her finger all the way to the funeral directors before he had thought to ask for it back. He would save that story for a later date and slip the family heirloom onto Flora's finger.

'There now,' he said with a smile, 'you're mine.'

CHAPTER 7

FLORA

I am betrothed to John Reginald Marshall. Flora chanted the words to herself all the way home on the bus. Soon they would be Mr and Mrs Marshall. Flora Marshall. The name had a certain ring to it, better than boring old Flora Jones any day of the week. She would give up Fine Fare and live with her husband in Grove Road and be a housewife in her own house. An actual married woman. A bit like her mother, only much more hip, with more friends and interesting wallpaper. Oh! A hostess trolley – that was a must. And a fondue set. There would be parties and fun and lots of outings. The girls at school would be so jealous, – her and Jonny M, who'd have thought it?

What a birthday! The best day of her life by far. After what had been the yummiest Knickerbocker Glory she'd ever tasted, John had ordered Irish coffee to celebrate, and later, there had been an almost proper kiss in the shadows near the bus stop. Soon there'd be a lot more than just kissing going on. Finally, there would be actual bonking, or was that just for sluts? Anyhow, there would be plenty of how's-your-father, hanky-panky. Only one month to wait and she'd be the woman she's always wanted to be. They had already agreed, the wedding should take place before the end of the school summer holidays, so John could start the new academic year without interruption.

Back at home, she burst into the sitting room where her parents were watching *Opportunity Knocks'* – 'It's make-your-mind-up-time!' said a perma-tanned Hughie Green. Not wishing to compete with the clap-o-meter, Flora turned the sound down and stood in front of the screen to make her announcement.

'Marry?'

'Mr Marshall? Your old geography teacher from St Margaret's? The one with the dicky leg?'

'It's John. And for your information, he got his leg in the war.'

'Is this another of your daydreams? Because let me tell you, marriage is to be taken seriously.'

'It is serious. We are in love and we want to be together forever.'

'For goodness sake, Flora!' they chorused.

She stopped listening and just watched their mouths; like a pair of goldfish, they went on and on. They would say what they always said, 'Why can't you be normal, mix with people your own age? What about those nice young men at Fine Fare, the lads on cheese and cold meats? Surely there's someone…'

The chances of anyone at Fine Fare wanting Flora as a friend, let alone a love interest, had been apparent on her first day. Just as it was in school, people tended to forget her name and ignore her unless they wanted something. She knew she wasn't overly pretty or clever, and she had no special talents, but how was it possible to be almost invisible? Until John came along, she'd lived her life in the half-dark, and from what she could gather, so had he. They were two odd socks making up a pair; much better together than apart.

~◦◦◦~

The following day at work, Flora rolled her left sleeve up to the elbow and used exaggerated hand movements to try and attract the attention of her Fine Fare colleagues. The expanse of flesh definitely gave the twinkling diamond extra emphasis, until the manager asked her to wear her overalls properly. When no one had noticed by late morning, she leaned over the cheese counter and held out her arm in a 'you may kiss my hand' kind of gesture.

'Hey, Kevin, what do you think of this then?'

'Eh? What am I looking at?' He was more interested in rearranging the Double Gloucester.

Flora waggled her fingers and said, 'my solitaire diamond engagement ring, silly.'

'Oh. Who's the unlucky victim?' He began spearing Dutch flags into a globe of Edam.

'Don't be mean. I'm engaged to be married to Mr John Marshall, actually.'

'Who's that? Not that old pervert in the brown suit?' He smirked and called over to the fish counter, 'Hey, guess what? She'd only gone and got herself hitched to that weirdo.'

'Who, Jake the Peg?'

Flora hurried back to her trolley, trying to block out the running commentary on how they'd never manage a standing-up shag and what their kids were going to look like. She had planned to hand in her notice and work the statutory two weeks, but now she felt like leaving right away.

At closing time Flora threw off her overalls in the cloakroom, applied a dab of lipstick, then undid her ponytail and brushed out her hair; John would be waiting. Thank goodness. He was the only nice, decent person in her life. Marrying him was going to be the start of a wonderful new beginning and everyone at Fine Fare could shove it up their bums! As she walked out into the sunshine, John stepped forward and she took his arm. Safe at last.

After a pleasant half-hour in the park, enjoying the late afternoon sunshine and a flask of tea with her fiancé, Flora caught the bus home. Her parents were already sitting at the tea-table laid with plates of egg mayonnaise and salad. Mum had her going out lipstick on; that was a sign if ever there was one. She spoke in a calm voice and told Flora the best thing she could do was write John a letter, explain she'd been swept up in the moment and return the engagement ring.

Then Dad said his piece through gritted teeth. So far as she knew he had never actually lost his temper completely; somehow he managed to sustain the tipping point, like an opera singer holding a note. 'He's taking advantage, Flora. He was your teacher for goodness sake! If the school wasn't closed for the summer holidays, I'd have a word. What's he think he's playing at?' His face was so red, he looked like a Swan Vesta. 'And not even the courtesy of asking for my permission.'

Flora concentrated on the geometric patterned wallpaper behind his crimson head. If Mum wasn't there, he'd probably be more reasonable, but they always closed ranks in the end.

'Where's he live, eh? Give me his address and I'll teach him some manners.' When he thumped the table his knife bounced and chimed on his water glass like a musical full stop and the baton of persuasion passed back to her mother.

'It's utterly ridiculous, Flora. Marriage is a commitment for life. God knows how hard it can be. You have no idea of the sacrifices I've had to make.'

'Well, you shouldn't have got yourself up the duff then, should you?'

'That's enough, Flora!' Dad's was dangerously close to exploding.

'Well, it's true. At least I'm marrying for love.'

'Love? You don't know the meaning of it.' Mum reached for her cigarettes, which signified the end of her involvement so Dad would have to take over. It wouldn't be the end until they got their way.

Well, not this time.

She stood up and glared at them. 'I don't care what you say. He's the love of my life and we're getting married. So there!' She shoved her chair out of the way and as she left the table, flipped up her plate of salad so two halves of egg loaded with mayonnaise and a sprinkle of paprika skidded and bounced across the table and landed in her father's lap.

'Come back here, young lady,' he shouted after her, 'we have every right to stop this nonsense until you're twenty-one, do you hear me?'

Flora thundered up the stairs while he shouted after her, 'You're making the biggest mistake of your life.' Then as she threw her bedroom door shut, she heard, 'We'll have no part in the proceedings. Pay for everything yourselves and suffer the consequences.'

'Good riddance to bad rubbish!' Flora shrieked through the closed door.

'And you can forget about those driving lessons,' came the last shouty reply before the dining-room door slammed shut.

Flora didn't care. John was Romeo to her Juliet and her parents' disapproval made their love tryst all the more intoxicating.

~~~

John's marriage proposal and then her parents' pleading had given Flora a taste of something deliciously empowering. She was flying high for the first time in her very average life and taking charge of her own destiny. Only last week she had read something about it in *Nova*; no longer allowing herself to be shackled to the expectations of a patriarchal society, nothing was going to stop her from becoming an independent woman. No matter what anyone said, she'd be Mrs Marshall by the end of the month.

It would have been nice to have friends to share the news with and show off her engagement ring. Ava Schulze and Mary O'Connor had been the girls she was closest to at school, thrown together as for being either Jewish, Irish or fat with freckles. They were outsiders with no other options, rather than being actual friends. When Ava and Mary had got on to secretarial college, neither had suggested keeping in touch. Flora briefly imagined seeking them out, then recalled the time she'd seen them on a wet Saturday afternoon a few months ago. She had been about to cross the road and take shelter from the rain in the Milkbar, then spotted them sitting in a window booth, each with a boyfriend and a Knickerbocker Glory, laughing together and having fun without her.

Mrs Peters, next door but two, was young and friendly; she was always good for a chat. There was so much Flora wanted to ask about married life and hoped to be invited in for a cup of coffee and a proper conversation, but Mrs Peters opened the door with her headscarf on and the baby already in his pram, about to go out.

'Ta-dah!' Flora held her left hand out and moved it around slightly to catch a twinkle.

'Engaged? Let's have a look. Oh, lovely!'

'John says it's a real diamond and quite valuable,'

'So, who's this John then? It's all a bit sudden, I didn't even know you had a fella, how did you two meet?'

'Oh, I've known him for ages, he used to be at St Margaret's.'

'He's one of your old teachers? Isn't that a bit, you know, a bit funny?'

The baby started crying and Flora stepped back while his mother manoeuvred the Silver Cross out of the front door and bounced it down the front steps.

'I really like him, he's –' Flora paused while Mrs Peters jiggled the pram in a soothing rhythm and the baby quietened down. 'He's kind and clever. A real gentleman.'

'I'm sure he is, love, but shouldn't you experience a bit of life before you get lumbered with a husband and babies and all that? Don't get me wrong, I love little Jimmy, but this is it now. I could have had a career, you know?' Flora looked at the baby, now sucking his thumb. Did John want children right away? Perhaps they should talk about that. 'And what about boyfriends? You don't have to marry the first man you meet, especially your old teacher. What age is he?'

'Early thirties,' Did that sound younger than thirty-three? 'But age doesn't matter to me, we get on so well together. I can't wait to be married.'

Mrs Peters took the pram's brake off. 'Well, it's not always going to be a bed of roses, love. Just think about the other end, when he's an old man and you're having to clip his toenails.' She began to wheel away and called over her shoulder, 'In this day and age you have the world at your feet.'

~◦◦◦~

At home, Flora had taken to eating her meals on a tray in front of the television after work. It suited everyone and helped to keep the household tension at a bearable level, but weekends were more difficult. John said he had to keep those days free to prepare for her moving in, so, apart from working a half-day shift on Saturdays, she had nothing much to do except shop for a few things for her wedding and dream about the future.

For as long as she could remember. Flora had imagined her wedding day would be in a church. She'd have a huge white dress with a fabulously romantic lace train, carried by a clutch of pretty little bridesmaids. Most important of all was the headdress, simple yet sophisticated with a lacy veil which would be lifted by her adoring groom. On seeing her face, he would gasp at her beauty and fall in love with her all over again. It would be the day when she truly shone. Her day. Dad would have tears in his eyes as he gave his speech, and although Mum would try and outdo her with the biggest, brightest hat imaginable, she would also make a magnificent three-tiered wedding cake and decorate it with silver bells and sugar roses.

Without Dad to pay for a fairytale wedding, she would have to make do with the Coventry city centre registry office. She had already been there on the bus one Saturday afternoon to familiarise herself with the surroundings and was surprised to learn that the old building had once been a medieval royal palace. At least that was something. She had watched a newly married couple stand on the steps to pose for an official photograph. She noted that the bride was wearing a simple, neat pale pink dress and a pillbox hat and the groom was in an ordinary suit and tie. By the look of things there was a baby on the way. Although a traditional wedding dress would be a bit over the top, at least the future Mrs Marshall would still qualify to wear white.

After looking through a few magazines and several 'trying on' shopping trips, Flora settled on a white cheesecloth maxi; not a real wedding dress, but a nod in the right direction. Later, she would dye it purple for when they holidayed at the seaside or when John took her to a fancy restaurant.

Flora spent her last Sundays at home in her bedroom. With August's gap in the rain and a gentle heat, she had the window open and the curtains half-closed. She had borrowed the greatest romance of all time from the library. Not her usual choice but these days all she could think about was love. She prepared to read *Romeo and Juliet* by imagining herself in an exotic far off land, somewhere like the Mediterranean where olive trees scaled surrounding hills and goats foraged for fragrant herbs. A beautiful house with a terracotta roof, her bedroom with a balcony and below, a fountain played in the courtyard. A footpath, lined by peach and lemon trees, lead to a beautiful garden that tumbled down to a sparkling blue sea. Flora enhanced the perfect setting for Shakespeare's lovers with her new transistor radio. Nearly all the songs in the charts seemed to speak to her, *The Wonder of You*, *In the Summertime*, *All Right Now*. And soon, Stevie Wonder's *Signed, Sealed, Delivered, I'm Yours* would be coming true too.

After skimming over almost incomprehensible dialogue and discovering the world's most romantic play ended in a double suicide, Flora went back to practising her signature. She was still unsure whether to go for the full Flora Marshall in flowing script or a more indistinguishable scribble, best used for cheques or letters of complaint. When her mother's conversation in the garden below caught her attention, she turned down the radio to listen. As usual, Jane from the bridge club had popped over for a natter while 'the men' played golf.

'I don't know where we went wrong with her. He's old enough to be her father, and a crippled one at that.'

A cluck of sympathy floated upwards, then her mother said something more quietly, 'wasn't the prettiest…no special talent…shop-girl.'

Yes, it was insulting, but she'd heard it several times already, usually over the garden fence or whispered into the telephone. Gossiping, even about her own family's scandal, was one of Mum's favourite pastimes.

It was satisfying to know her parent's turmoil continued. With less than two weeks before the wedding, Flora knew she could still change her mind at any time, but she wouldn't. In fact, she may as well pack a few clothes and take them round to John's house. She'd be moving in soon and she was sure Dad wouldn't offer to drive everything over there for her. Still catching odd words from the conversation below, she pulled a suitcase out from under her bed, only recently returned from what would now be known as the last ever family holiday.

Flora squashed two drawers worth of clothes into the case and closed it by sitting on the lid and bouncing until everything was squashed enough to allow her to close it. The deadweight was a bit of a surprise. She thumped it step-by-step downstairs, half-hoping she'd attract her mother's attention. On the pavement, she tried her best to adjust her lopsided walk to a nonchalant stroll and arrived at the bus stop having worked up a sweat. No matter, she enjoyed the sensation of almost leaving home this way, suitcase by suitcase. Ever since John had given her his address in the hope of a holiday postcard, Flora had wondered what his house looked like. Grove Road sounded really nice, probably on a street lined with trees, grass verges and a park at the end. When she'd asked, John had said it was a 'Perfectly serviceable three bedroomed, semi-detached.' So in addition to the leafy avenue of trees, it would probably have a garden front and back.

It was a shame John hadn't asked her father's permission for her hand in marriage. It might have made things easier, but then again, Dad still wouldn't have agreed. She wondered who would be good enough for his 'Pickle'. If he thought Kevin on the cheese counter was better than John, then he had no idea about anything. Flora looked into the front gardens along the bus route. Cosy houses, net curtains, happy families. It had never been like that in their house; although it looked like everyone else's, there was always tension. Mum pushing her out of the way. Both of them wanting Dad's attention. And Dad, weak and loving, trying to keep the peace but always siding with Mum in the end. She was better off out of it.

The novelty of almost eloping began to wear thin after changing buses three times, then struggling along Grove Road, looking for number ninety-three. The only house in the street without a bay window stood out like a sore thumb and while all the other homes were painted soft pastels or a crisp white, number ninety-three still had the old grey pebble-dashed render. From the outside it reminded her of the time she visited her grandmother, who was dying of tuberculosis; while Mum had a good cry, she had been made to wait in the car which was parked on the road. She had gazed at Nan's grey house and thought how sad it looked, even before it became a place of death. John's place was neglected in the same way and, like Nan's, the front gate was only wide enough for a coffin, not a car. Never mind, she'd soon have the whole place looking lovely. Pastel pink would be nice, with white window frames.

Whenever Flora had thought about married life, she pictured her home to be the nicest in the street. Neat, pretty and welcoming.

And when her new friends and neighbours would come for morning coffee and a slice of homemade Victoria sponge cake, she imagined a doorbell with a soft chime, like the one at home. In reality, she had to clang the metal letterbox flap while avoiding catching her fingers. Never mind, that could be sorted out as well.

'Flora! What on earth's going on?' John didn't seem as delighted as she'd hoped.

'I thought you'd be pleased to see me.'

'Well, I am, of course, but –', he pointed to the suitcase, 'what's all this, I thought we agreed to wait?'

'Oh, no I just thought it would be easier to bring a few things over, I don't think Dad's going to help me. He's still hoping I'll call it off.'

'Well, alright. You'd better come in but you can't stay long, it wouldn't be correct.' He lifted the suitcase into the hall and led the way into the sitting room.

While his back was turned, Flora undid the third button on her blouse.

'John?' It still gave her a thrill to say John instead of Mr Marshall.

'Yes?' he said, as he sat down in an armchair.

She cat-walked towards him while working her lips into a seductive pout. She'd been reading *The World's Most Sexiest Women*; Christine Keeler really was an inspiration.

She straddled John's lap and pulled off his glasses.

'Steady on!' he gasped.

She was sure he'd caught a glimpse of her knickers.

'What's the matter, don't you fancy me anymore?' she said, pleased with her husky voice.

'You know I do, it's just that –'

'So prove it.' She grabbed his tie and pulled him into a kiss but he swerved just enough to give her a glancing peck on the cheek.

'I'm sorry, Flora, but these papers won't read themselves,' he said, while pushing her off his lap.

'What's up with your mojo?'

'There's nothing wrong with my so-called *mojo*, thank you very much.' He took his glasses back and stood up to straighten his jumper. 'Remember, we have an agreement.'

'Yes I know, but we'll be married in no time.' Flora reached for her handbag. 'You're such a square.'

'Well, maybe I am, but we are going to do things properly, as you well know.'

⁓᷅᷄᷅᷄⁓

The idea of not doing things 'properly' was about all Flora could think about. She couldn't wait to put into action what she'd only ever read about in books; Lady Chatterley's Lover being the most informative, followed by an armful of frothy romances. Although the unlikely couplings of a hero and his beloved were frustratingly light in detail on the actual act itself, they all guaranteed a happy ending. Her latest library book about a misunderstood buccaneer and an innocent milkmaid was a prime example of their situation. John even had a passing resemblance to the open-shirted swashbuckler on the front cover.

Re-reading the sexy parts of books was one thing, but actually doing 'it' was going to be something else. Just as soon as she was Mrs Marshall, she would be claiming her conjugal rights. Despite her initial disappointment, in many ways she was glad they were having a stay-at-home-honeymoon. So far as she was concerned, seeing the sights on the Isle of Wight would come a very poor second to doing 'it' morning, noon and night for a whole week.

At the soonest opportunity, when both parents were out of the house, Flora would telephone the Family Planning Clinic for an appointment. There was no need to invent a boyfriend or answer awkward questions; as a bride-to-be she qualified for a bare-bottomed turn in the stirrups, fair and square. She had already handed her notice in at Fine Fare. Just five more days of shelf-stacking, then married life and freedom would be hers.

CHAPTER 8

JOHN

John's concerns about sharing his home with anyone other than his mother's ghost faded into insignificance compared to the idea of sharing a bed, let alone the act of lovemaking. The matter was made all the more disturbing by Flora's astonishing display of wantonness when she had brought her suitcase to the house. Until then, sexual intercourse wasn't something he had ever envisioned doing.

As a soon-to-be-wed, all the fervour and anxiety of his youth flooded back as though it were yesterday: the giggling, whispering girls, the bullying boys. The Limping Spectacle. The one and only girlfriend at university, who lasted all of two dates. Now that he had the prospect of a fully functioning, long term relationship, it was somewhat daunting. Furthermore, although Flora was undoubtedly a virgin, recent events suggested to him she would be a very willing sexual partner, which was both thrilling and terror-inducing in equal measures.

He was plagued by the conflict of sexual arousal and the possibility of irrevocably terrifying his bride, or worse still, disgusting her. Without any practical experience, he had a desire to be well versed in the whole procedure. With this conundrum weighing heavily on his mind, he went to calm his nerves at the allotment, where he weeded around 'The Girls' and checked their cheerful blooms for aphids until a solution came to mind. To his relief, he concluded, as with most things, all the answers would be revealed in a book. An afternoon's foray to Coventry City Library would answer everything.

In preparation for deflowering both himself and his bride, John plunged into the necessary research with all the determination of a final year student. He didn't expect there would be a reference section on sexual intercourse, but the medical shelves yielded several useful textbooks. With morbid fascination, he became side-tracked and scribbled notes from *Systemic changes during the menstrual cycle* and then dedicated several hours to *Ideal marriage: Physiology and Technique*. He skipped over *A Right Choice of Marriage Partner* and *Good Psychological Attitudes*, and focused his attention on *A Vigorous and Harmonious Sex Life*. By the end of the day, John had a good grasp of the essentials and felt empowered by his bulging notebook.

Finally, National Geographic gave him the assurance that not all men looked the same naked; some of them, particularly in some of the more remote tribal communities, were even poorer specimens than he was. With his newfound knowledge, John became more nonchalant about the act of consummation; if it didn't go to plan, the marriage vows 'for better, for worse' guaranteed he would have 'until death' to sort it out.

CHAPTER 9

FLORA

Lying down on the floor and breathing in helped Flora to do up the last buttons on her new high-waisters. She should have bought a bigger size but at least they made her look curvy rather than just podgy. She already knew she would pair them with her new rainbow coloured tie-dyed shirt, knotted just above her tummy button. After a generous helping of Rimmel's Hide 'n' Heal miracle spot camouflage, she powdered her face and then worked on creating sophisticated eyes with aqua shimmer and a double coat of mascara. A critical inspection in the wardrobe mirror told her that with the addition of her duo orange and white sling-backs, she was now a real somebody. If she'd had them, she would have topped off her look with a pair of large gold hoop earrings to let everyone know it was a special day, the beginning of a womanly adventure.

The journey into the city centre was uneventful. She didn't see anyone she knew and there were no dishy men on the bus to impress with her new look. Walking past shop windows, she caught a glance of her reflection which prompted her to pull her shoulders back and push her chest out. Walk like a goose, look like a swan. She turned down a side street and found the discreet Family Planning sign emerging from a respectable shrubbery. The neat white wooden gate clicked behind her and with a fluttering heart, Flora hurried up the steps to the front door.

As she entered the waiting room, a line of washing-day-weary mums swivelled on their wooden chairs to assess the newcomer. By the way they clutched at handbags or raised magazines higher they conveyed a certain disapproval. She knew what they were thinking; she'd heard the stories relayed by her mother's gaggle of eighteen-hour-girdle-wearing friends. The term they favoured was strumpet. A pretty mini-skirted girl walking past often earned Dad a sharp dig in the ribs. 'There's a strumpet, looking for trouble,' her mother would mutter. The same went for the dancers on The Benny Hill Show; strumpets, every one of them.

'Yes?' The receptionist's powdery lipstick contracted into a cat's bottom grimace. Instead of looking up, she shuffled things around on her desk, clearly more important than yet another strumpet looking to leap on the free-love bandwagon. Flora took in the old lady's twinset and imagined she was wearing starched bloomers under her tweed skirt.

'My name's Flora Jones, soon to be Mrs Marshall actually. I have a two o'clock appointment.' She tried to force a smile, but it wouldn't come out.

'An appointment isn't a forgone conclusion. First, you must complete this form and provide proof of your forthcoming marriage or, failing that, a birth certificate. She didn't say 'to ascertain your morality,' but she may as well have done.

With the form completed, Flora handed over the registry office papers confirming her impending marriage. With indisputable evidence, old Mrs Starchy-Bloomers allocated Flora a changing room that was more like a broom cupboard; no windows, just a coat hook and a wooden stool. On the back of the door were the instructions to strip completely naked, put on the gown provided and wait for a nurse. '*Do not leave the cubicle unless accompanied by a member of staff*', was underlined and Flora wondered what would happen if there was a fire. She stood in the dim light for what felt like hours until a bustling nurse, who seemed too busy to speak, took her to an examination room.

While still acclimatising to lying on a chilly plastic mattress, the nurse wrenched Flora's legs up and prised her knees apart. Before she could work out what had happened, her timid pink virginity was on display to the world. The nurse then plonked a clipboard on her chest as though she were a table, snapped on an angle pose lamp to spotlight the star of the show and left the room.

Alone once more, Flora wondered if anyone had ever been left lying like that overnight, perhaps giving the cleaner a nasty shock in the morning. While still immersed in the scene of a traumatised cleaning lady, she was startled when the door was thrown open by a man with an air of importance and a white coat.

'Hello.' Flora half extended her hand, thinking they should introduce themselves in what was, after all, a very intimate matter, but the doctor was tapping the clipboard with his pen while reading her chest-supported notes and didn't seem to notice. The examination proceeded in silence, and all Flora gleaned from the experience was that someone had cold hands and an even colder metal speculum.

Back in the waiting room, with the excesses of medical lubricant seeping into her knickers, Flora perched on the edge of a wooden chair and tried to ignore what sounded like tut-tutting coming from a couple of matronly women on the other side of the room. Finally, a disembodied voice called Miss Jones and a brown paper bag was thrust through the serving hatch. She had hoped for more clarity, but there was no one to ask, so she stuffed the package into her bag and hurried out.

On the way home Flora made a detour to the shops to make a final decision on her wedding night nightie. A Barbara Cartland bride would wear a satin negligee and not much else, so the dashing new husband could fumble with the flimsy ribbons and let it fall to the ground. However, the nightwear department at Woolworth's was more for the budget conscious bride, less satin, more rayon. On a previous visit Flora had narrowed it down to a pink baby doll or a white midi. But now that she was carrying the gateway to paradise in a brown paper bag, she could see without question that the white midi was far more sophisticated. It was quite pricy, but an alluring nightie was the cornerstone for a happy marriage.

Having made the purchase and eager to get started, she hurried home, pushed past her mother, who still wasn't speaking to her and locked herself in the bathroom. Inside the brown paper bag, there was a leaflet entitled, '*On Your Wedding Night*', a tube of spermicidal jelly and a blue flying-saucer shaped box containing a Dutch cap. The flying saucer also carried a step-by-step guide for use with a disquieting diagram of a woman sawn in half.

Flora read everything twice before copying the pose of an intrepid explorer with one foot on top of a mountain summit, or in her case, the loo seat. She poked a finger into her already traumatised vagina. Clearly, it had had quite enough interference for one day and the slippery little hat wasn't keen on going in either. After the fourth time of fighting its rubbery determination to flip open at the point of entry, she changed tactics and lay on the floor. It was a bit of a squeeze, but with her head right under the sink, wedged between the Harpic and the Ajax, she imagined she was back at the clinic, only without the stirrups, and braced her feet against the side of the bath. With a simple twist and a quick poke, she eased the diaphragm into position.

As much as the bathroom would allow, she then walked around, bent at the waist and sat on the edge of the bath, expecting to feel something alien inside her, but she felt nothing at all. In the mirror she saw a girl who was well on her way to becoming a woman. She undressed and slipped on the white satin midi nightie. With pouty lips and what she hoped were come-to-bed eyes, she pushed her breasts up and together, into a plausible cleavage. Boom bang-a-bang!

CHAPTER 10

JOHN

John stood in front of the bathroom cabinet and examined his features for any tell-tale signs of malaise. Perhaps he was a little pale, and maybe his forehead conveyed a slight temperature; whatever it was, it was unsettling enough to reach for the Milk of Magnesia. He swigged a couple of mouthfuls straight from the bottle while glancing warily at himself and doubting all the while that his condition was a medical one.

When the discomfort failed to abate, he considered Mother's other cure-all treatments; cod-liver oil for insides and iodine or calamine lotion for external use. A quick swig of cod liver oil would probably do no harm, but after that, he would have to reconsider the root cause rather than the symptoms. It was nothing he had eaten, of that he was certain, and he hadn't come into contact with anyone with a cold. On his way back downstairs, he sat on the bottom step and studied Flora's suitcase. He hadn't touched it since its unexpected arrival the previous week and now as he looked at it, the strange sensation in his abdomen grew stronger. He had left the case just inside the front door, not because he didn't know where to put it, but because he felt that once he carried it upstairs, his old life would be over forever. There would be noise. Interruptions. Sharing. The suitcase invading the hall was an embodiment of Flora.

Mrs Higgs had already gone. After a grand finale with a feather duster, swiping away the last of his bachelor days, she held forth for a good fifteen minutes on the blessings of female company. She had known John since he and Mother had moved to Grove Road in 1943, watched him growing up and seen Mother through her final illness. Now that John had found himself a young lady she could move to her sister's place in Lyme Regis, knowing he was settled. As she handed back her keys and dabbed a hankie at a few stray tears, the last meaningful link to Mother took off her pinny, closed the front door for the last time.

Things were moving along apace. In two days, John would be a married man, destined never to sleep alone, eat alone or enjoy entire Sundays with a good book, uninterrupted. The last couple of times he'd met Flora for a walk, her chitter-chatter had been slightly irritating. John put it down to pre-wedding nerves, but at the back of his mind he worried that he didn't altogether know her very well. He had been in a rush to secure his bride before she met someone else. Had he really thought the whole thing through?

On the other hand, what if she changed her mind? He had read the small print; until Flora signed the register, she could nullify their agreement. Even after that, if the marriage wasn't consummated, there would be grounds for annulment. Looking at it from the vantage point of a single man, living alone, retiring alone, with no family to take care of him in his old age, it would be his loss much more than hers. He didn't need Mrs Higgs to tell him he was lucky to find a lovely young lady. Given his track record, she was his only likelihood of marriage.

While the discomfort of relinquishing tranquillity still plagued him, he grabbed the suitcase and dragged it upstairs with a degree of difficulty. Flora had hauled it on and off three buses to get there and he hadn't even offered her a cup of tea. Feeling slightly ashamed, he vowed to make amends. He would empty it so she could refill it with whatever else she needed and carry it from her house, himself. Never mind the parents. Maybe it would even soften the almost-in-laws' resolve if they witnessed how attentive he was to their daughter. From what Flora had told him, he knew this wasn't likely, but all the same, he needed to ensure his bride would follow her belongings into his house without a hitch. While he was at it, perhaps he should add some of the homely touches Mrs Higgs had been on about.

Perhaps some dahlias? Mother liked to have them on the mantelpiece in a vase. He usually only cut them whenever he was going to the cemetery to visit her grave. But yes, dahlias would be a good idea. And perhaps he should clear some space; Flora had said there was only one more suitcase of things to bring over. In the bedroom, he combined his socks, pants and vests into one drawer and put all his other clothes into another, leaving Flora a larger share of the chest of drawers. There was already plenty of space in the wardrobe. He wasn't a snappy dresser and made do with two suits, almost identical shades of middle management brown, one newer than the other.

Feeling a little self-conscious, he opened the suitcase lid and gazed at the rainbow of colour. Without thinking, he picked up the first item and held it to his nose. Lemon and lime? Violets? Fresh cut herbs? Whatever it was, it gave him a strangely erotic sensation that wasn't altogether unpleasant. Should he decide where everything would go or leave that to Flora? In the end, he managed to force all the clothing into the largest bottom drawer, leaving almost an equal amount of space for the next load. A pair of white patent leather go-go boots lay at the bottom of the case. John gingerly picked them up between finger and thumb and pushed them under the bed, out of sight.

In the bathroom, he cleared a shelf in the cabinet. Women's things were far more complicated these days; Mother never had half of Flora's paraphernalia. Hairbands and ribbon, cosmetics, lotions and potions. No doubt there would be yet more fripperies to come, probably enough to create an avalanche every time he opened the cupboard. Annoyed at something he had only imagined happening, the stomach gurgling started all over again.

Halfway through his lunchtime sandwich, John hit on an idea. Chalk boxes. He had always brought them home if no longer required in school. They were sturdy yet small, easy to slide in and out. A row of them in the cabinet for Flora would look like a nice thoughtful gesture and better still, keep her knick-knacks under control.

With his wife-to-be's belongings stowed upstairs, he walked from the bedroom to the bathroom and back and could hardly tell the difference, in fact the household topography appeared unaltered. Flora was already almost moved in and he felt alright about it. What a relief. Tomorrow he would take the empty suitcase to Fine Fare and accompany her home on the bus for a refill.

ᴗᴔᴔᴊᴊᴗ

That's that then, John. My last day. I've packed in working forever!' Flora chatted non-stop about her future as a housewife, the pleasure of handing back her Fine Fare overalls and how she wouldn't miss her work colleagues one little bit. 'They'll be turning up for work tomorrow while I'll be a lady of leisure. I might even have a lie-in just to prove it.'

John was hardly listening. Although he was happy to know she had in fact finished work and had therefore taken another step towards marriage, the imminent meeting with her parents was all he could think about. Perhaps it would have been wiser to have asked her father's permission before proposing to Flora? He had considered it at the time, but why would anyone wish their daughter to marry a cripple? The Limping Spectacle was not a catch, everyone knew that.

'So, should I address your parents as Mr and Mrs Jones? Yes, of course I should.' He briefly had the notion they might like him to address them as Mother-in-Law, Father-in-Law, goodness knows where that idea had come from. It must have been before he had proposed, when he had grudgingly accepted they would have to go round for Sunday lunch as a married couple or worse, spend Christmas day as a family. If one good thing had come out of their disapproval, he was sure they wouldn't be doing that in the foreseeable future. Conversely, his fear now was more of a confrontational nature.

'Flora, love, do you think perhaps my meeting your parents might exacerbate the, er, situation?' On seeing her blank expression he clarified, 'Aggravate them more than they already are.'

'Well, Dad's still going ballistic at me all the time and Mum's stopped speaking. I don't suppose they'll invite you in for a cup of tea, if that's what you mean.'

'Should I perhaps wait for you to pack the suitcase and bring it out to me?' Yes, he was a coward, but he didn't think he would fare well with someone going ballistic.

'Dad's best friend, Robert, lives opposite. He'd probably go ballistic as well if he saw you standing outside,' said Flora, then to John's relief she added, 'Probably better if you wait at the end of the road, at the bus stop or something?'

'Good idea. I'll wait for as long as it takes.' He hoped he had hidden the relief in his voice and silently congratulated himself on letting Flora arrive at the right decision herself.

As they alighted from the bus, Flora kissed him on the cheek and said, 'I'll be back in a jiffy,' and hurried away with the empty suitcase.

He looked around and hoped anyone who had 'ballistic' tendencies might already be at home preparing for their evening meal. Having to loiter in a strange neighbourhood without a newspaper to read made him feel conspicuous. He stood closer to the bus stop, looked at his watch then glanced up the road with the pretence of waiting for an intercity. But when the number seven pulled over for him to climb aboard, John was forced to step back and wave the driver on. With 'Bleedin' hell' still ringing in his ears, he crossed the road to wait in what he hoped was a nonchalant stance in the shade of an overhanging laburnum.

The avenue of trees and smart detached houses was a surprise to John. He had presumed as a shelf-stacker, Flora would have lived in a two-up, two-down terraced house on an estate. Realising how little he knew about his bride made his stomach churn in what was now a familiar sensation. How would she feel about living in Grove Road? He had presumed she'd be delighted to have a three-bed semi, but clearly, number ninety-three was going to be a step down. Was this testament to how much she was enamoured with him or was she just not materialistic? It didn't matter all that much in the long run, but the idea she might be in line to inherit her parent's house and have financial independence was both attractive, yet disempowering. No matter, he'd leave that for another day. Getting Flora to the registry office was his primary concern, and with that thought, he hurried across the road to meet his bride-to-be who appeared to be carrying another heavy suitcase.

'Sorry, it's the books,' Flora panted.

'Books are always a weight worth heaving.' Books, eh? Flora was a surprise a minute. 'What are the tomes of delight within?'

'Eh?'

'What books have you packed?'

'Oh, you know, all the classics.'

For a moment, John wondered if he was in a parallel universe and Flora had indeed brought a catalogue of classics. But when she reared off a list including The Princess Bride, Her Gypsy King, Dora Dances to Paradise, he smiled at her and said, 'Well, that little lot should keep you out of mischief,' and gladly hauled the frothy nonsense onto the bus. As he waved her goodbye from his window seat, he felt safe in the knowledge that he did at least have the upper hand when it came to literary choices.

Later that day, John unpacked the second suitcase and found space for Flora's bouquet of romantic novels on the bottom shelf of the bookcase where they would be obscured by the sofa. He then wandered around the house adjusting the soft furnishings for a more feminine appeal; a slightly more jaunty tilt of a lampshade here and a plumped up cushion there. Tomorrow was his last day as a bachelor, and he now felt ready. Marriage was going to be the new life he never thought he would have. Yes, it would require sacrifices, but it would pay off in the long run.

~~~

Having excessive nasal tissue made John snore so loudly, he sometimes woke himself up with a start, but this was different. He switched on the bedside light and sat up. A pounding in his chest. A sense of panic that he had forgotten something. Was it anything to do with the registry office? A quick mental list, ticked off on his fingers and double-checked reduced his heart rate to a near-normal level. Of course. Now there were two mouths to feed. He would have to buy extra groceries, then in the future, he would have to provide some sort of housekeeping allowance so Flora could do the shopping. The idea of setting aside a proportion of his wages was giving him a 'suitcase-in-the-hall' sensation, but it was a necessary part of being the husband. He understood that and considered the division of labour between husband and wife to be a clear boundary. He was all for rules and timetables; the absolute certainty it brought was going to be just one of the many benefits of having a wife. He would sort everything out in the morning.

John began the day by writing the milkman a note requesting two extra pints a week and made a note of the additional cost. He then hurried out to buy a few staples, enough to get them through the first few days of marriage. A honeymoon-at-home should have one or two treats, an extra packet of fig rolls would go down well, and a large tin of Prince's ham should see them through; good for sandwiches and a salad. Before reaching the counter, he placed a few bottles of Double Diamond in the basket for his wedding night. Then he tried to think about what a bride should have. Flora had ordered a Babycham at her birthday meal, but perhaps sherry would be more befitting the occasion. Amontillado seemed to be the cheapest but with a name like that, there could be anything in there. Better stick to something British. Bristol Cream had a nice reliable ring to it. Pricey, but she'd only need a drop or two, and they could save the rest for Christmas.

After unpacking the shopping and making himself a quick meat paste sandwich, John set about the final touches and consulted Mother's collection of recipe books. Within a couple of hours, he had everything written down in an old school exercise book, with a cross-referencing meal plan. Then from memory, he recreated Mother's housework rota at the back of the book, mapped out just like a school timetable so it was easy to see exactly what was what, and when. With everything set out in writing and Mother's absolute oracle, Mrs Beeton, for back up, he felt confident he had everything under control.

With Mrs Higgs no longer cleaning twice a week, his outgoings were reduced, however, with two mouths to feed, the cost of household groceries would have to go up. John wrestled with the equation for some time, before justifying that one pound, fifteen shillings and sixpence would suffice for a housekeeping allowance. Decimalisation was just around the corner, so he would have to review it then, in any case.

John double-checked his 'to do' list and tidied everything away, ready for Flora's arrival. With preparations completed, he spent the rest of the day in glorious isolation, savouring the last few hours as a lone bachelor in his own home. Tomorrow he would set off early, collect his bride-to-be from the end of her road and together, they would travel to the registry office. After the minimum of fuss, they would be husband and wife.

CHAPTER 11

FLORA

Flora locked herself in the bathroom, cut the price tag off her cheesecloth maxi with a pair of nail scissors and slipped it on. After adjusting her cleavage for maximum effect, she took a moment to admire the simple, yet tasteful design and the fact the length made her look more mature. Sophisticated, even. Humming the bridal march, she tried to drown out her father's voice on the other side of the door.

'*Tum, tum-tee-tum.*'

'You're making the biggest mistake of your life.'

'*Tum-tum tee tum,*'

'No-one else'll want you when it all goes wrong. You don't even know the man.'

Makeup next. A lovely new lipstick, Tangerine Dream. Black double-lash mascara and plenty of it. '*Tum-tum tee tum-tum.*'

'What about his family, eh? Have you even met them?'

By the time she had wrestled her hair into a sort of updo, he had changed tactics.

'Please think about it, Pickle,' he said in a soft voice, 'I only want the best for you.' And then, 'Look, I know it hasn't always been easy, but you're my special girl, can't we at least talk about it, eh? Come on, Pickle, what do you say?' Silence. 'You're breaking your mother's heart. She's beside herself.' Flora knew this wasn't true; two weeks ago, her mother had barged into her bedroom while she was reading *Two Hearts Eternal* and measured up for new curtains, saying it would make an ideal sewing room.

Flora rubbed a smudge of stray lipstick off her teeth and gave her reflection a winning smile. Satisfied with the whole ensemble, she stuffed her makeup into her handbag, slipped on her sandals, unlocked the bathroom door and barged past her father.

'Listen to me, young lady!' He thundered down the stairs behind her, 'If you leave this house, you'll not come back!'

Mum was already on the doorstep, arms folded, tight-lipped.

As a final act of defiance Flora picked all the marguerites from the terracotta pot in the front garden and slammed the gate behind her. With the fizz of endorphins spurring her on, she carried the flowers in a speedy bridal march, past the twitching curtains to the end of the street where John was waiting. It was the most exciting, daring thing she'd ever done.

༺⚹༻

The marriage ceremony at the registry office was over in less time than it had taken to get there on the number twenty-two. With strangers for witnesses and no other guests, Flora signed the register. Goodbye forever, Miss Jones, shelf-stacking spinster. Hello Mrs John Marshall, housewife and one day, mother of two.

Afterwards, she linked arms with John to pose for an official photograph on the registry office steps, holding the wilting marguerites in front of her like a prized trophy. With two hours to wait until opening time, they took a stroll in the municipal gardens and later, sat on a memorial bench with a cup of tea and a Chorley cake from the refreshments stall.

For their celebration meal, Flora had chosen a pub called The White Hart, not for the menu but because it sounded romantic. Despite a brisk twenty-five minute walk from the gardens, they were one of the first customers and found a window seat overlooking the evening rush hour. They were served by a spotty waitress with dirty cuffs.

She sauntered over, took out her pad and pen and gave them a quizzical look.

'We'd like chicken in a basket for myself and my good lady wife,' said John nodding at Flora, who giggled and squirmed in her seat.

The waitress was impervious. 'Sauce?'

'Oh, yes, undoubtedly. Flora love, sauce?'

'I should say so,' said Flora, giving the waitress an exaggerated wink. Still nothing.

'And a Babycham,' added John.

'Is that twice, or do you want a shandy?' The waitress smirked at her own joke.

Flora didn't care. She was a married woman, and soon, it would be her wedding night. She knew what to expect, thanks to the wanton Lady C and her lover. Very soon, John would unclothe her and lie her down, so he could kiss her navel while she lay *'quite still, in a sort of sleep, in a sort of dream'*.

<hr />

Fortified by two bottles of Babycham, chicken in a basket and a slice of apple pie with custard, Flora was keen to move on to after the afters and said, 'Let's get a taxi, husband!'

'Whatever for? Have you lost the use of your legs now that you're a married woman?' He held out his elbow and said, 'Shall we?'

Flora linked her arm through his for the walk to the bus stop. They took seats on the top deck. With Flora sitting next to the window, John leaned over to point out landmarks along the way. 'And if you look past the cemetery where Mother is, my allotment's up there. Home to 'The Girls'. Flora nodded, all the while thinking how strange it was to call a few dahlias 'The Girls'. As he went on to describe Taratahi Ruby's prize-winning features, she smothered a twinge of jealousy. He'd never commented on her own appearance with half as much enthusiasm.

As they turned to walk down Grove Road, Flora hoped to catch the eye of a neighbour, someone who would become a future friend. With her white dress and wedding bouquet, it was obvious to all who cared to look, she was the new bride arriving at number ninety-three. Perhaps there would even be one or two couples already waiting in their gardens to give her a cheery, welcoming wave.

To be fair, at that time in the evening, Coronation Street would be on. Never mind, there was plenty of time to get to know everyone. As soon as John was back at work, she'd organise a coffee morning, invite all the Grove Road housewives and catch up on the local gossip.

'Ah, here we are, Mrs Marshall,' said John, giving Flora a gentle nudge in the ribs, 'Your new home awaits.'

She eyed the small area at the front of number ninety-three; where everyone else had a small lawn or flowerbeds, there was just plain grey concrete that blended almost seamlessly with the house. It was big enough for a few pots to jolly it up, and some hanging baskets would look nice too. Pink and white geraniums to go with what would soon be freshly painted pebble-dash. John opened the gate and ushered Flora through, then reached past her to put his key in the lock.

'You have to lift me over the threshold,' she insisted.

'Do I really?'

'Of course! Everyone knows it's seven years bad luck if you don't.'

'That's just superstitious nonsense,' John's hand was on the small of her back as though to guide into the house.

Flora wondered if she might cry and bit her lip. The groom scooping up his new bride and carrying her into her marital home was symbolic and the most romantic thing, ever. It was something she had dreamed of since she was a little girl.

'Alright, come here then, just this once.'

He picked her up after a second attempt, staggered to get his balance before shuffling backwards into the house and put her down too quickly on the mat inside. His arms had felt boney; the idea of finally seeing what lay beneath Jonny M's brown suit suddenly became a little intimidating. The most she'd seen of his body was on a picnic in Spencer Park a couple of weeks before. When he'd rolled his sleeves up, his forearms had reminded her of celery sticking out of a shopping bag.

'Welcome to your marital home,' said John, gesturing around the front room. She'd seen it only once before, but it had seemed much bigger and brighter then. A well-stocked bookcase dominated the space, taking up almost a whole wall; a few oversized volumes spilt onto the plain brown carpet. With cream coloured Anaglypta wallpaper and a beige sofa, it was a man's house that needed a wife to make it pretty.

John sat down on the sofa and patted the space next to him.

'I'll just pop to the loo first,' said Flora and dashed upstairs.

The bathroom smelled of mildew and coal tar soap; it would need a freshen up too, a feminine touch. Flora stood on tiptoes to see her face fully in the mirror; it would have to be moved down. She was going to be busy, but that's what wives were for – to take care of home comforts. Once she was settled in, she'd have her proper dressing table, with a pink velvet seat and she'd set about making everything else just so. Before she knew it, she'd have a redecorated home, a wide circle of friends and everything would be perfect.

Back downstairs, John was carrying a tray of bottles and glasses from the kitchen. 'How about a nice glass of sherry? It's Bristol Cream?'

'Oh, rather.' She tried to pronounce it *rah-ther*, the way Madeleine Carroll did in *The Prisoner of Zenda*. If only I smoked, she thought, I could light a pink cocktail cigarette and lounge on the sofa in a sophisticated pose.

John poured himself a bottle of beer and held up his glass and said, 'Here's to us! Health, wealth and happiness.'

Flora took a quick sip of her sherry. It tasted like the smell, only stronger. Should she say something back, another toast perhaps? Difficult to know.

Silence.

'*A Double Diamond works wonders, works wonders!*' she sang and winked at John, then wished she hadn't.

Nerves.

The idea of lying naked next to an actual man was about to become a reality. She had never had the sort of relationship with her mother where she could ask about the facts of life. Only on one occasion had they come close. When she was thirteen, Mum had muttered something about 'the curse' and left a bulky brown paper bag on the end of her bed containing a packet of Dr White's and a sanitary belt. Once a month thereafter a new packet appeared, with a hand towel draped over it for modesty.

John sat next to her on the sofa, seemingly content to gaze into space. She couldn't think of anything to say either. The clock ticked on the mantelpiece. She fiddled with her sherry glass.

Somewhere further up the street, an ice cream van chimed the first few tinny notes of Greensleeves. An ice cream on a summer's evening would be a real treat. She'd suggest that tomorrow, during their after-dinner stroll. The silence was making her edgy.

She moved her hand onto John's knee and cleared her throat. 'It's been a smashing day, hasn't it?' she said.

'It has,' agreed John. 'I hope that photograph comes out alright – seventeen shillings and six is an absolute scandal.'

'Yes, but we'll have two copies. One for us and one for Mum and Dad.' Flora hoped her parents would come round to the idea of their marriage, perhaps when a grandchild was on the way; then she could give them the picture and everything would slot into place. 'It'll be a lasting memory, for richer, for poorer, until death do us part,' she added.

'Now, there's a thought.' John drained his glass.

'I'll get a nice frame from Woollies,' said Flora, half to herself.

When the late evening sun began to set, John stood up to put the light on and did a pretend yawn. Flora laughed nervously and topped up his Double Diamond too fast so there was too much froth.

When he took a sip, it left him with a thin white moustache. She imagined licking it off.

Eventually he said, 'You'd best go and get ready then.'

Oh my giddy aunt, here we go! She hurried out of the room, hoping she wasn't blushing. In the bathroom, she opened a new bar of lavender soap to wash her underarms – no one likes a sweaty bride, she'd read that somewhere. She brushed her teeth for the full two minutes, gave her hair a hundred strokes, then put on her new satin midi nightie. After inspecting herself in the wardrobe mirror, she re-applied her lipstick.

She could see from a pile of National Geographic magazines and an alarm clock on the bedside table that she should take the opposite side, so she climbed in, stifling a nervous giggle as she arranged herself in an alluring pose.

The wait was longer than she expected. After at least twenty minutes, she heard John in the kitchen, rinsing their glasses at the sink. He locked the front door and slowly mounted the stairs. As he pushed open the bedroom door, Flora tried pouting and looking out under her lashes at the same time, but he switched the light off before he could appreciate the combined effect or the way she'd spread her hair on the pillow.

He undressed in the dark, then pulled back the blankets and climbed straight on top of her. He covered her face with clumsy wet kisses, simultaneously smearing her with perspiration from his upper lip.

'Now, let's get on with it shall we, Mrs Marshall?' he slurred. With a clammy hand, he fumbled under the bedclothes for the hem of her nightie and pulled it up to her waist.

The sharp pain of penetration dulled into a numb throb as John relentlessly jabbed into her. With hot, beery breath and gargled grunts, he sounded more like a frenzied animal fighting with itself than the thoughtful lover she had hoped for.

And then, with one final thrust, it was over.

He collapsed on top of her and soon began to snore. Flora struggled to breathe as she lay in a patch of cooling semen, still waiting for the exquisite moment to begin.

~ මෙම ~

The next morning Flora opened her eyes to see her new husband already sitting up in bed, deeply engrossed in a magazine. She watched him for a while and wondered what he thought about their wedding night.

From her point of view, it was hard to reconcile Lady C's *'strange thrills rippling inside her'* or Jane Birkin's scandalous sighs of *'Je t'aime'* with what had taken place. Until the moment John began grappling with her, she had truly believed that making love would be pretty sensational. So why had it felt more like being thwacked repeatedly in the privates by a small rodent? She looked at the man wearing the same patterned pyjamas as her father's, buttoned right up to the neck, and wondered if he'd been doing it wrong or whether it was her. There was only one way to find out.

'Morning, John.'

'Ah, there you are.' He was in a cheerful mood and didn't seem the least disappointed with his wedding night. 'Just in time for a cup of tea.'

'Oh, yes please, that would be lovely.' Flora was thrilled, as she'd never had a cup of tea in bed before. She imagined after a nice cuppa, they could have another go at doing 'it'; in fact, they had a whole week to practise before the new school term began and John had to go back to work.

'Off you pop then,' John nodded towards the door. 'We may as well start in the way we mean to go on.'

'Oh, I –'

'And when you come back up, I have a little something for you.' John looked pleased with whatever it was. The idea of the 'little something' being whatever lurked in John's pyjama trousers excited Flora. She leaned over and kissed him on the cheek before scrambling out of bed. As she headed downstairs, she heard John call after her, 'Don't forget to warm the pot,' and wondered if it was a euphemism. So far as she was concerned, her pot was warming up nicely.

While the kettle built up a head of steam, Flora arranged the cups and saucers on a tray. With the teapot's knitted cosy and a full jug of milk, they'd have everything to hand for a second cup. Afterwards.

'Here we are,' said Flora, 'tea for my husband.' She liked saying, husband. It gave her a feeling of togetherness, where anything was possible. Marriage was going to be a wonderful adventure.

'Thank you, my love.' John patted his side of the bed and said, 'Sit here.' He leaned over and opened the bedside drawer. Flora was surprised to see him retrieve a large book. 'I have it on good authority that everything you'll need to know is within these pages.' He tapped the hardback cover.

'Is that the present, or is there something else?'

'This is the present. I think you'll find it very useful.'

Flora took the book. Perhaps it was a fuller, more explicit version of '*On Your Wedding Night*'.

'I want you to know, it's my intention to be a good husband and do all I can to help you settle in. This book belonged to my dear mother.' He picked up his teacup and took a sip

'*Mrs Beeton's Book of Household Management.*' Flora read the title aloud and opened the book at the index. While only half-listening to John's enduring childhood memories – of how his mother would ask him to look up certain things, she double-checked the contents page but couldn't see anything about marital bliss or husbands.

'Mother used to call Mrs Beeton's her second bible,' said John.

'It says here it was first printed in 1861, that's over a hundred years ago, isn't it a bit –.'

'If it was good enough for Mother, I'm sure it's plenty good enough for you.'

'But, I –'

'I'm only thinking of you, my love. Have a look. It's full to the brim with helpful advice.'

Flora half-heartedly flicked through a few chapters.

'And I've something else.'

Flora looked up from the section entitled, *'Managing Your Household Staff'*, hoping to see something frivolous: a love token perhaps. But John was waggling an exercise book at her.

'I've written everything down in here, so you don't have to think. Shopping, meals, a rota for your housework, even telephone numbers. Everything you'll need, to save you asking.'

'Save me asking?'

'Here you are, see, today is Wednesday. Breakfast. Boiled egg and two slices of toast, but–' He held up a finger. '…At the same time, you'll need to prepare my packed lunch. Sandwiches and an apple. Cheese. And don't go fussing with the crusts, I like them left on. Dinner is at six and there, you can see if you follow the chart, we're having shepherd's pie tonight with tinned peaches and Carnation Milk for afters.'

Flora tried to think of something to say. John knew she had qualifications in cookery and home economics. She had planned to surprise him with new and exciting recipes; she had seasonal menus, special occasion dishes and a party buffet already worked out.

'I've even written the corresponding page numbers for Mrs Beeton's recipes. Oh, and here you can cross-reference her excellent tips on housework.'

'Well, that's very helpful, but I thought you –'

'Now, as today is our honeymoon, I won't require the packed lunch. No need for the rustle of greaseproof paper, eh?' He nudged her as though he'd just cracked a joke. 'So, you can just make them at lunchtime, say twelve-thirty, ready for one o'clock – you do like cheese, don't you?' He turned a few pages and added, 'And, hey presto! The housework rota. See? I've already worked everything out for you.'

Flora had imagined her role as a wife to be more Christine Keeler than Hilda Ogden. Then much, much later on, she would be the mother in the Peter and Jane books. The main reason she had endured the Family Planning Clinic was so they could have fun without the burden of domesticity. Then in a couple of years time she'd have a girl, then a boy and then, after they moved to a house with a proper garden, they'd get a dog.

'But I thought you said you had a cleaning lady. Mrs Higgs?' Flora finally managed to finish what she'd been trying to say.

'Oh no. She's well past retirement age; she only stayed on after Mother passed away because she felt sorry for me. And I have you now,' he said, taking her hand. 'My little wife.'

CHAPTER 12

JOHN

When someone muttered 'Dirty Old Man,' through a knothole in next door's fence, John hardly flinched – as The Limping Spectacle he had heard far worse, and if that was in reference to his marriage to Flora, so be it. He'd never liked the neighbours in any case. At least he could now dispense with their annual sherry party, where the men bored on about football and the women simpered over plates of vol-au-vents. It would take more than an opinionated neighbour to spoil what had always been his favourite time of year; Autumn Term and the start of another academic year. A fresh influx of pupils was always a highlight at St Margaret's.

Although he was still on his honeymoon-at-home, John had been on his way to the cobblers when he had heard the derisory comment. Taking his trusty brown lace-ups for new soles was all part of his cherished back-to-school ritual. He received a louder 'Pervert!' on his return, but he barely registered the insult and hurried indoors. In a quest to continually improve his delivery of the curriculum to new pupils, he had a new and exciting idea to create an aide memoir. Before anything else he would to draw couple of diagrams, mapping out the academic journey through the excellent *Fairgrieve and Young* series. Later, he refilled his fountain pen, packed his briefcase for the following day and went to bed satisfied that life couldn't be much better.

The much anticipated back-to-school day had started in a pleasant way, especially considering it was Flora's first day as a fully-fledged housewife. She had prepared his breakfast with a perfectly timed boiled egg, made his packed lunch and put it in his briefcase on schedule and then, the part he liked most, she had waved him off at the door, just like Mother. It felt good to walk to the bus stop, knowing he would return to a home cooked evening meal and a pleasant conversation with his wife. Marriage certainly had been congenial so far.

As was his habit, he alighted from the bus with time to buy his newspaper and be at St Margaret's fifteen minutes earlier than the rest of the staff. Experience had taught him this was the easiest way to avoid dreary conversations on the highs and lows of each person's summer holiday. By the time they arrived in the staffroom, he would be sitting by the window with his newspaper, clearly engrossed, so that a simple nod and a smile from him would suffice without offence.

He hung up his coat and before pouring himself a cup of tea, perused the staff noticeboard. He skimmed over the sports fixtures pinned beneath '*Autumn Term 1970*' and focussed on the academic timetable. It must be a complicated business, putting the whole curriculum onto one large sheet of paper, although little seemed to change from year to year. All the same, someone had made an admirable effort in rewriting the whole thing with the odd amendment here and there. He already knew where he would be for his first lesson – the same as usual, but it was always a good idea to check. He stepped a little closer, scanning the columns for his name while taking pleasure in the copperplate handwriting.

'Ah, Mr Marshall, I've been looking for you.' A Scottish accent gave away the presence of the school secretary. He always thought of her as an ally; she had been so helpful throughout Mother's illness, even telephoning him at home to see how things were over the Christmas holidays. Granted, they had drawn the line at first-name terms, but when she said the headmistress wanted to see him immediately, the usual softness in her voice was missing.

When John knocked on the study door and entered, he was surprised to see the four people gathered around the headmistress. He vaguely recognised them from prize-giving as governors of the school. However, this time the meeting was devoid of handshakes. Complaints had already been received. His immediate resignation was required. And no, he didn't need to work his notice; Miss Simpson had agreed to come out of retirement until a replacement was found.

Within an hour of getting off the bus, John was on its return journey to the suburbs, all the while gripping the handle of his briefcase so tightly his knuckles were white. What on earth had taken hold of him? Marrying Flora without ever imagining there would be consequences. Yes, she was an ex-pupil of the school, but she had left two years ago, he hardly remembered her from that time. There certainly had not been any funny business. Not in the slightest.

He hesitated before walking back down Grove Road. This was a sorry business but perhaps there was an answer. What if he divorced Flora and claimed temporary insanity? No. The governors had been quite clear and furthermore, they would not provide a character reference. His resignation from St Margaret's would have to be explained to any future employer. Facts would be checked. Maybe he could try and get a job in a private school; they were far more bohemian, weren't they? If he couldn't teach geography, perhaps he could start afresh with a different subject, but he would still need a reference. The whole debacle was more devastating than a tectonic slide.

As he neared home, still worrying how to tell Flora the news, it dawned on him that perhaps she had only married him because he was a teacher – there was a certain kudos to that. How would she take to being the wife of a disgraced ex-teacher? Still trying to frame the news into a palatable sentence as he opened the front door, he caught the soft crooning voice of Nat King Cole singing *When I Fall in Love*. Mother's music.

It seemed almost unbelievable, but there was Flora, waltzing around the sitting room with her eyes half-closed, hugging a cushion. A ridiculous spectacle at any time of day, but at half-past nine in the morning, when there's work to be done and…

'Oh, John! You started me.' Flora froze in mid-twirl.

'What in heaven's name are you doing?' He strode over to the record player and lifted the arm. Despite his hand shaking with anger, he was careful not to scratch what had been one of Mother's most treasured possessions.

'I, I was just –.' Flora clutched the cushion.

'Well, that's all very fine, you prancing about like a half-wit while I've just been given the heave-ho.' He heard himself speaking without thinking.

'What do you mean the heave-ho?'

'I've been sacked, or asked to resign is the way they put it.'

'What?' Flora gasped, 'Sacked from school, like, expelled d'you mean?'

'Yes, Flora! Your intellect sometimes astounds me. I have been asked to resign my position as geography master on account of marrying an ex-pupil of the school.'

'Me?'

'Of course you, you imbecile.' John sank into his chair and took his glasses off. 'I'm sorry, I'm a bit overwrought. I can't quite believe it.'

'Neither can I. What did they say?'

'They said, it had been brought to their attention that a teacher from St Margaret's has shown a grave misjudgement and if they were to retain their reputation as custodians of young ladies, they would have to make an example of him.'

'Him?'

'Me. And if I didn't resign forthwith, I would be sacked in any case.'

'Oh, no,' Flora sat on the arm of the chair and tried to put her arm around him.

'Don't do that. It's your fault we're in this position.'

'My fault?'

'Yes, yours. You with your short skirts. Laughing at my jokes. You turned my head, but I never imagined you'd cost me my job as well.'

'It wasn't just me.' She jumped up. 'It takes two to tango, John.'

'That's a typically inane rationale. It might take two, but you led me on. I was alright on my own. I should have stayed a single man.'

'And I should have stayed at Fine Fare!'

'Teaching was the love of my life.'

'I thought I was the love of your life. That's what you said. You said I would make you the happiest man alive by marrying you.' When he didn't say anything she added, 'Do you want me to leave? So you can go back to what you love.'

John took out a handkerchief and blew his nose. 'Put the kettle on, will you. I could do with a cup.'

While Flora was in the kitchen, John tried to think more clearly. Of course he would have to get a job, but would he be able to stay in a teaching capacity? How should he go about finding out? He'd heard about the labour exchange, but as someone who had always had a career set out for him, he'd never had to think about it.

'This is a fine state of affairs,' he said when Flora carried in his cup of tea. 'I won't get a reference, not now. Despite the fact I've taught at that school for years. They wouldn't even afford me the dignity of working my notice.'

'What'll you do?'

'Without a reference I can't teach.' His voice cracked, and for a moment he feared he might actually cry. 'Geography is all I know.'

'Shall I go back to Fine Fare? That'll bring in seven pounds, fourteen and six a week.' Flora spoke in a quiet voice, as though it was the last thing she wanted to do.

'Have you no sense? Do you expect me, as a newly married man, to send my wife out to work while I sit at home? No, thank you very much. I think you've done quite enough damage already.'

John drank his tea quickly then passed the cup and saucer to Flora without a word. As soon as she took it back to the kitchen, he went upstairs to change. He needed to think, and he couldn't do that with her around. He would go to the allotment and dig things over.

~~~

With the sun on his back and birds singing nearby, John walked along the row of dahlias cupping each bloom in his hands in the search for thrips or aphids. It was always soothing to inspect 'The Girls', in just the way Mother had taught him. Satisfied that there was just cause, he went into the shed and mixed up a solution of soap and oil. Squirting each frilly pompom in the face had a calming effect, and gradually, he relaxed enough to think straight. Perhaps leaving St Margaret's wasn't so bad. Maybe he could find something he enjoyed just as much as teaching. Or perhaps he could become a geography academic and write a book; goodness knows he was well informed, his whole life had been focussed on the subject. He could fill the gaps in the *Fairgrieve and Young* textbooks; he even had a couple of diagrams he had prepared for the autumn term, it would be a shame to let them go to waste.

'Is that you, John?' A woman's voice interrupted his thoughts. He'd come to the allotment for a bit of peace and quiet, but now he'd have to get involved in pointless chitter-chatter. He turned to face the old lady. One of Mother's old gardening friends

'Hello, Mrs Coombe, how are you?' He forced a smile out of respect for his mother.

'Mustn't grumble, but my hips are playing up. I'm not much good at the allotment these days; I'm hoping he'll take it on before too long,' she nodded to a small boy picking peas a few vegetable plots away.

'Your grandson, I presume?' He pictured the boy tripping over and screaming, so the old woman would have to rush off to pick him up.

'Yes, that's my little Martin. I've six altogether. He's the youngest.' John's heart sank when she began calling the child over. 'Marty! Marty! Come and say hello.'

They watched the boy run towards them, still clutching a handful of pea pods. 'He's such a darling, this one. Loves spending time with your Granny, don't you? Say hello to Mr Marshall, Marty.'

How could he get rid of them, what if she asked him why he wasn't at work? Did she know it was the first day of term? As a grandmother of six, almost certainly.

'Hello, Mr Marshall,' said Marty and held out his spare hand. John was slightly taken aback but shook it anyway, noting how small and hot it felt but not knowing what to say. His only interaction with children was from the front of a classroom, with distance and authority. The boy smiled toothily and added, 'It's a pleasure to make your acquaintance.'

'Isn't he a scream?' Mrs Coombe hugged the boy to her side. 'He's only just turned four and already he likes to do everything properly, he has better manners than most adults, don't you think? Such a little charmer!'

'He certainly is, Mrs Coombe.' He knew he should ask questions, show an interest, but he had other things on his mind. 'Well, I'd better get back to –' his voice trailed off, hoping that was a sufficient signal.

'Yes, indeed. Come along, Marty. Let's get those peas picked, shall we? Mr Marshall seems to have a lot on his mind.' She gave him a half-smile and a tilt of the head, indicating a sort of sympathy. Did she know about St Margaret's? She hadn't mentioned Flora, so hopefully it was just that look he was used to seeing from his mother's friends, who probably saw him as some sort of tragic bachelor, nothing more.

John watched the little boy lead his grandmother back towards the pea canes and then hid in the shed until he saw them pack up and leave the allotment a few minutes later. With no one else around, he continued to exterminate pests with added vigour.

CHAPTER 13

FLORA

The thought of going back to work at Fine Fair wasn't all that awful. Moving back home to Mum and Dad and not being married to John wouldn't be so bad either. On top of John losing his job, life as a newlywed was already a huge disappointment. Instead of pre-wedding nerves, she had post-wedding nerves. Had she made the biggest mistake of her life, just as Dad said, or was this just a bumpy beginning? Like the young girl in *The Rose and the Rogue*, could she turn things around and become the mistress of her own destiny?

The honeymoon-week-at-home hadn't been dreamy or romantic – not even just fun. She had expected day trips, the cinema or and evening at the theatre. She had planned to cook a candlelit dinner. And in between outings there would be bubble baths with Babycham on the side, and sex. Lots and lots of sex. Surely that was the reason people married, so they could have as much sex as they wanted without suffering the consequences?

Instead of spontaneous bonking in the middle of the day, or even just passion at daybreak, followed by breakfast in bed, John kept his pyjamas buttoned up and his hands to himself. She hadn't even seen him naked, let alone caught a glimpse of his 'thingy'. He seemed to wait until she went to the bathroom, then by the time she was out, he'd be fully dressed with hardly more than a 'good morning'. At night he'd wait until she was in bed, then switch the light off, change in the dark and keep to his side of the bed. Was that shyness or trying to avoid doing 'the deed'?

Looking back on their honeymoon-at-home, the highlight had been when John took her to the allotment where they shared a flask of tea while he weeded around 'The Girls'. Then, on the return journey, he suggested a detour to the cemetery to visit her posthumous mother-in-law's grave. Later at home, she had tried her best to lure him upstairs by wriggling her way onto his lap while he read *World Sciences*.

'I need the pleasure of your company upstairs.'

'What for?'

She winked and said, 'You know what for'. When it became apparent he had no idea, she added in a low voice, 'Hanky-panky.'

'Flora, really. It's four o'clock in the afternoon.'

'Yes, I know. Just in time for tea. You can have a slice of me with your cuppa, how about that?'

'Where on earth do you get your ideas from? Those romantic novels have filled your head with fantastical nonsense.'

Flora was beginning to wonder if perhaps the joy of a sexual union was indeed nonsense, but if that was the case, why did everyone go on about it? Certainly the few minutes' experience on her wedding night had been a let-down, but surely after the first time, it would be better. Shouldn't they be 'at it like rabbits'?

Ever since the wedding and even more so since he'd lost his job, John's mojo was on the turn. Sex would have to wait. It was hard enough to get a word out of him, and when she suggested perhaps inviting people for drinks or a dinner party to cheer him up he had been unreasonably rude. So far, she hadn't met any of his friends, and now it appeared the university chums he had told her about were ancient history: he hadn't kept in touch with any of them.

She had assumed John's friends and neighbours would become part of her new life, just like Mum and Dad's busy social calendar, she had expected several events a month. Was it her job to create a social life? Where were the regular meet-ups? Shouldn't there be a card night at a neighbour's house or drinks at six on a Friday?

She had tried saying cheerful hellos or good morning to the neighbours on her way up to the corner shop or the bus stop, only to be met with an odd look she couldn't quite decipher. She would have to go to each house and introduce herself. Around ten-thirty seemed best, when an invitation to come in for a cup of coffee would be most likely. Then she could reciprocate, and before long she'd have built up quite a morning routine. Getting to know the husbands and socialising as couples could wait until John had a job and was feeling more settled. The adjoining house seemed the best place to start, number ninety-five.

'Hello, I'm Flora Marshall, your new neighbour.' An older lady half opened the door. Her tightly wound rollers were covered by a hairnet and pinned down as though a high wind might undo all her good work.

'Flora is it? Well, best of luck to you, love.' She had the local newspaper and a pen in her hand, as though she were about to do the crossword.

'Thank you,' Flora said and pointed to the paper, 'Is that today's? I usually do mine in the afternoon. Yesterdays was tricky, wasn't it? I only got four, how about you?'

'I keep going 'til I finish it. Like everything, it takes effort.'

'Oh yes, absolutely. I was wondering if you'd like to come round for coffee sometime, maybe do the crossword together?'

'No offence, but I prefer to keep to myself.'

At the house on the other side, she would use a longer opening line, and although already feeling a little crushed, she would try to sound more friendly, less desperate. An unsmiling woman in her late thirties answered the door.

'Hello, I thought I'd pop round and introduce myself, seeing as we're going to be neighbours.' She held out her hand. 'Flora Marshall, John's new wife.'

The woman barely shook her hand, letting it drop after a brief gesture of politeness. 'I know who you are. I hope you know what you're doing; a young girl like you, wedded to a chap like that?'

The conversation didn't get anywhere close to a coffee invitation. It was unlikely they'd ever be friends, but what did she mean, referring to John as 'a chap like that?' Was it because he was a bit older than her or something to do with his limp? No-one knew John like she did.

Perhaps she needed to relax, let friendships form more naturally. Maybe wait for a chance to do a good deed; return a dropped glove or a straying child. Whenever she was out, she looked for ways to connect. Opening doors for overloaded housewives, offering to carry shopping, helping the elderly across the road. Nothing seemed to go further than an occasional 'thank you' without meaningful eye contact.

Without friends to visit or special dinner parties to prepare for, Flora spent her days rearranging the kitchen cupboards and clearing out the pantry. She had learned not to touch any of John's things after she'd pulled all the books out of the bookcase to rearrange them in alphabetical order. How was she supposed to know they were already in specific categories? The same went for the furniture. After moving the sofa and heaving the television to a more central point in the room, John had insisted on putting it back to how it was.

It soon became apparent that only the kitchen was her domain and for that, she dipped into her savings and bought a plant for the window sill and a tin of pale pink emulsion. It took three coats before the horrid wallpaper would stop grinning through but finally, she had the beginnings of a house that, one day, would feel like home. She knew without even asking John, she would have to live with the rest of the dreary decor until he was back in employment. Hopefully, with a new job and a steady income, she could create the pretty home she dreamed of and John would go back the Jonny M she thought she had married.

CHAPTER 14

JOHN

John had never worried about keeping up appearances with the neighbours, but he had told Flora that leaving the house each day as though he were still going to work, would be for the best. He said it was for her sake, but in fact, it served him very well to have an excuse to go out every day and stay out. With a packed lunch in his briefcase and not expected home until teatime, he had the freedom of an invisible job.

Spending entire days in Flora's company had begun to lose its charm during their week-at-home-honeymoon. She seemed to have a constant need for attention, interrupting his reading for an aimless conversation or to suggest they go out for a walk with no purpose or destination in mind. Additionally, he hadn't allowed for the noise another person in the house would make. Mother had never been one for playing the wireless, but Flora had her transistor radio tuned in to popular music channels almost continually. They had agreed she could play her music in the kitchen with the door shut if he was reading in the sitting room, but he could still hear it, even then.

By his reckoning, a five-day to two-day ratio comprising a working week and a Flora weekend would have been perfectly tolerable. But with no job to go to, the thought of impending days, weeks, possibly even months of concentrated domesticity was almost a worse fate than the whole St Margaret's debacle.

Without the routine of paid employment, John designed a timetable for himself which centred around Coventry City Reference Library. A whole morning was taken up in the reading room with the newspapers. Starting with the locals and moving on to the national broadsheets and weeklies, he scrutinised the Situations Vacant advertisements. In an old exercise book he divided the pages into columns to accommodate notes, with a shortened code for the specific newspaper and details of role as advertised, application details and a small space for the date sent. The afternoons were for writing letters to any of the possibilities. When the work was complete, he sifted through the envelopes, ticked them off in his notebook and posted them in a city centre letterbox before heading home.

To break up the day he went for a walk at lunchtime and found a suitable place to eat his sandwiches. He soon worked out the best park benches and found a bandstand for when it was raining. If the situations vacant pages had been particularly sparse, he filled in time by visiting a couple of museums. Once, when he was feeling particularly wretched, he slipped into the Odeon cinema. He bought a matinee ticket; it didn't matter what was showing, undoubtedly it would be a load of old rubbish, it was more for an escape from reality. As it happened, Zulu turned out to be most uplifting and left John feeling grateful he only had to find a job, not fight in the Battle of Rorke's Drift in searing temperatures while dressed in a bright red woollen overcoat.

After seven weeks' worth of job applications and a few interviews, he was finally invited to a second appointment with Franklin Union Insurance. The idea of asking people to pay for something that might not happen appealed to John, and he was good with figures. The fact that they were looking for an older candidate was to his advantage and when they said they didn't require any previous experience, it seemed to be almost too good to be true.

A few days later, when Flora propped the morning post against the breakfast teapot, John quickly sifted through the obvious bills and rejection letters to the only hopeful looking white envelope, and hurriedly opened it. With Flora leaning over his shoulder, he read the first few lines aloud. 'Further to your interview, Franklin Union Insurance would be pleased to offer John Reginald Marshall the position of Insurance Sales Negotiator.'

'Negotiator,' echoed Flora.

'Look at that, after all those years as a qualified teacher; it seems the real money is in insurance. I'll be earning two pounds and four shillings more than I did at St Margaret's. Isn't that something?' It was the first time he'd felt like smiling in weeks. 'And they want me to start on Monday.'

'That's such a relief. Shouldn't we celebrate? Do something special?'

'For once you're right, Flora.' He deserved a treat after the past few weeks.

'When Dad was promoted, we had salmon with mandarins in aspic and –'

'No need for any fuss, I think I'll just allow myself a day at home and put my feet up.' John got up from the table, 'Lunch at one? You can just serve my sandwiches on a plate.' He took his lunch box out of his briefcase and handed it to Flora before going into the sitting room. A whole day to read *The Geological Legacy of Angkor Wat* and maybe a bit of *Destroyed Civilisations*. South-East Asia really was a fascinating place.

CHAPTER 15

FLORA

Robert Dougall, the most handsome newsreader on television, had said good night in his reassuring tone, and now the weatherman was predicting a frosty November morning followed by a light drizzle. Flora came into the sitting room from the kitchen, plumped up her cushion and sat down on the sofa.

'Come on, hurry up.' She called in an upwards direction, to where John was changing the fuse in his bedside lamp. 'It's starting any minute now.'

'The weather forecast?' John appeared in the doorway, screwdriver in hand.

'No, you've missed that. Come and sit down; you have to watch it from the beginning.'

'I'm sure I don't.'

'John! You said you would. It's tradition.'

'By tradition, you're suggesting a pre-existing established –'

'Stop spoiling it. You said you'd watch it with me.'

Finally, the greatest show on earth was about to begin. For as long as Flora could remember, watching Miss World had been one of the few times she and her mother had shared a common interest. They had sat together, discussing the costumes and deciding who should win, all the while providing their own commentary. With a seasoned expert eye, they'd say, 'Oh, look at her earrings, much better this time' and 'Didn't the

Spanish one almost trip over last year as well?' John would be a poor substitute in that respect, but he would have to do.

'It's absolute nonsense, all those women titivating themselves, prancing around like prize ponies, and for what?'

'Well, there's nothing else on, so you may as well watch it.'

John picked up his newspaper, 'With all that controversy mounting up there might be some of those Women's Libbers protesting outside The Albert Hall. I didn't think I'd ever see the day when I agreed with that lot, but in this instance, they have a point.'

Flora had read the reports, seen pictures of the placards. '*Not Beautiful. Not Ugly. Just Angry.*' She'd overheard a few neighbours talking outside the corner shop that morning.

'Well, they're just a group of jealous women.'

'None of them have husbands.'

'That's what my Len says. Got no one to keep them under control.'

'Lesbians mostly.'

'They can't stop Miss World. It's just a bit of glamour.'

'Mind you, my Len gets all hotted up when those swimsuits come out.'

'Oh, naughty!'

With the latest controversy, Flora's opinion was divided. True, beautiful women jetting in from around the world brought a bit of glamour to everyday life, but was it fair they were only judged by their looks? If they included practical skills, cookery and dancing, ordinary people such as herself, who may, unfortunately, have a set of disproportionate vital statistics, could also be in with a chance. Between John's derisory comments and The Women's Libbers, her favourite show in the history of television seemed less exciting than usual. Why did women have to fight for everything? The right to vote, contraception, equal opportunities. Did beauty competitions undermine all that? She would have to think about it later.

The show opened with Lionel Blair and his dancers. All men, dressed in tight brown suits and frilly orange shirts. A disappointing start. Only Lionel was in time and none of the men were at all dishy. They didn't have winning smiles either.

'Look at them,' John snorted.

'I know' Flora imagined herself in hot pants and a sparkly boob tube, taking Lionel's part, with Pan's People for backing dancers. They would have done a much better job.

As the international beauties arrived on stage and had to navigate an excessive number of stairs in high heels and evening gowns, Flora willed them not to trip.

'Who are you going to pick? You have to choose someone to go through to swimsuits.'

'Must I, indeed?' John had slid a library book onto his lap and looked likely to open it.

'Come on, John. Join in and choose someone. It's meant to be fun. Let's say whoever chooses closest to the winner has their breakfast in bed tomorrow.'

'I've no desire to eat a meal in bed.'

'John!'

'Alright, Miss United Kingdom. If she says her hobbies include metal detecting, then there must be more to her than all that flouncing and warpaint.'

'I loved Miss Brazil's fabulous white feather boa, but Miss Ceylon has got that certain something. I can't decide.' If she'd been watching with Mum, they would have had a discussion on the merits of each contestant, but that was asking too much of John.

With the first part of the show over, Bob Hope was on the stage to entertain the audience while the judges made a finalist's shortlist and contestants powdered their noses. Flora imagined the buzz backstage. If she hadn't married John, maybe she could have been one of the makeup girls. In between her daydream of giving Miss Seychelles some winning tips in exchange for an exotic holiday, she half-listened to Bob Hope's patter.

He was rude about the Women's Libbers, then went on about Buckingham Palace's hospitality. Was that supposed to be funny? The Queen had to rule the entire commonwealth, bring up four children and manage household staff in all her castles and whatnot; even Mrs Beeton would have struggled to cope with that *and* put on a cocktail party. The audience wasn't impressed, no one was laughing. He moved on to the beauties who were changing into their swimming costumes backstage.

'But I don't want you to think that I'm a dirty old man, –' He certainly looked like one, 'Because I never give a woman a second thought. My first thought covers everything.'

A loud clacking sound. Something like fireworks came from somewhere at the back of The Albert Hall. Shouting and jeering.

The television stayed focussed on the comedian who had stopped telling awful jokes and was looking worried.

'What's going on here?' said John, leaning forwards.

Flora crouched next to the screen. 'Look! Someone's trying to get on the stage.'

Objects were being thrown. White smoke, or powder. More shouting. Jeering.

'Bob Hope's backing away,' said John. 'It looks like he's been targeted'

'Because he said the Queen's cocktails tasted like Bovril?'

'No, I assume it's the Women's Liberation lot, trying to make a show of themselves.'

'They're going to be on television,' gasped Flora, excited yet appalled. What about the beauty queens? They hadn't done their swimsuit round yet.

~∾∾∾~

'Well, well. The things you women get up to. Astonishing.' John had finished his breakfast and was reading the Saturday newspaper. 'It says those Women's Libbers last night were inside The Albert Hall all along. They had tickets and everything; we didn't see the half of it on television. Look at this photograph. Pandemonium.'

Flora leaned over his shoulder. 'Oh yes. It says they were throwing leaflets and flour bombs.' She tried to sound neutral, but the fizzle of excitement was almost too much to contain.

'Quite laughable, really.'

'It's not a joke, John. Women have rights. We should be equal.'

'Ridiculous,' John snorted, 'You'll be telling me you're as good as a man next.'

'Well, we are. If not better. Women work, cook, clean, have babies. Everything.'

'I'm sure they do, but that's because they can't do important stuff, like running the country. That's left to the men because you women don't have the mental capacity. It's not your fault. It's just nature.'

'If that's the case, why are the Women's Libbers even trying?'

'It's purely delusional. You're telling me a woman could be our Prime Minister?'

'Yes. Why not?'

'Don't be ridiculous. Burning your brassiere or dropping a few leaflets won't change anything. They've had their little protest. No doubt they'll be back in the kitchen by now, where they belong.'

Flora had just finished washing the breakfast things. Usually, she would go to the butcher's and get their Sunday lunch, then come back and make John a cheese sandwich while he spent the morning in the library. But maybe she had something more important to do.

'It looks like rain, John, don't get those library books wet.'

'Do you take me for some sort of imbecile?' He stood up, collected his books together and went to put his coat on. 'I'll be back at quarter to one.'

Of course he would. She could set a clock by John and his routine. As soon as the front door closed, she grabbed the newspaper. If Women's Liberation meant not having to stay at home, washing and ironing for the rest of her life, she wanted to know all about it. Just like the leaflets said, she wasn't beautiful or ugly. She was angry.

CHAPTER 16

JOHN

On top of the pay rise, another bonus to John's new job at Franklin Union was an added fifteen minutes to his daily commute. At St Margaret's he would have had to stay behind after school, marking homework so as to spin out the time before getting home. Now, with an eight-hour day plus travel time, he would arrive home with only another quarter of an hour to go before tea, therefore reducing the time to hear Flora's daily 'news' before they sat down to eat. What she got up to was rarely of interest but as a husband, it was his duty to lend a listening ear.

At St Margaret's, John had developed strategies to reduce pointless chitter-chatter to the minimum and presumed he would be able to do the same thing at Franklin Union. Much to his astonishment, social interaction with fellow office workers seemed to be part of the job. According to Roger, the office manager, it was a matter of absolute importance that he made an effort to get on with the girls in the typing pool if he wanted his quotations to go out in the same day's postal collection. It was also vital that he greeted Susie and Pamela on reception with a smile and that they received at least two or three compliments a week, otherwise his clients may not be dealt with as efficiently as others.

'Each?' asked John, aghast.

'Yes. Keep 'em sweet and everything'll be tickety-boo. And bung 'em something nice now and then. Flowers'll do.'

'Flowers?' Extraordinary to comprehend that he should have to be overly nice, just to get them to do their job.

'Yeah. Oh, and chuck a box of chocs into the typing pool and another to the telephonists - anything with kittens or puppies on the lid'll do it. One now, another at Christmas.'

'Um, is that really –'

Roger stopped in his tracks. 'Don't get me wrong, John, but you're not exactly Mr Charisma and you're no looker, so chocs it is. If you were more of the Paul Newman calibre, you could get away with a smile and a cheeky wink, but since your sales success depends on getting your prospect signed up pronto, you need the girls on your side. See what I mean?'

John nodded, hoping that was it.

'Now, as I'm responsible for handing out the live-wires, a bottle of something tasty'll do. Shall we say, one after your initial training and another around Easter? Scotch.'

'Right. And what is a live-wire?'

'That's the golden shot, John. Just a phone call to tie up the details and wham! Contract signed. Straight into your billy-bonus before you can say knife. Got it?'

'I think so, yes.' John totted up the price of success

'Now, I just need ten bob off you for the Christmas bash. The others are all paid up, so be a gent and bring it in tomorrow. I'll hand you over to Graham now and he'll get you started.'

'I don't think I'll be going to the –' John's words were in vain. Roger was already back in his office and Graham was waiting for him in the training room.

During his lunch hour, John ate his sandwiches in a nearby park and jotted a few likely compliments in his notebook - single words, so should Flora happen upon it, there would be no need for an emotional outburst. Hair. Smile. Outfit. Efficiency? Manners? Perhaps not. On his way back to the office, he popped into Woolworths and bought two bigger-than-he-would-normally-choose boxes of chocolates. The cost of nearly all box and no chocolate was a scandal, but as an investment, he couldn't do much better. To redress the slight twinge of guilt he felt on realising he had never bought Flora chocolates, or anything frivolous for that matter, he purchased her a Milk Tray Bar. With fourteen different flavours in one slab of chocolate, there was an excellent chocolate versus packaging ratio.

His morning training session had started with the importance of using a prospect's name, so he mustered all his reserves, stepped into the typing pool and asked each girl her name. No one could accuse him of being a slow learner. He was employing the rules and hoped that his small, fairly painless interaction would prove fruitful.

On arrival at work the next day he threw Susie and Pamela what he hoped was a charming smile and said good morning. He couldn't bring himself to pay them a compliment. He didn't know them and nothing of any merit seemed to stand out, but he heard the person behind him say, 'You're looking lovely today, ladies.' Perhaps he could have a go at that in a few days' time, when it might sound a bit more natural.

Training seemed to be pretty straightforward. There were strict rules on what he could or couldn't say or do, so it was just a matter of sticking to the manual. In a week, he would be allowed to speak to customers and soon after that he would be able to sign them up. Every new customer went towards his target and once the target number of customers had been achieved, he would begin to earn commission on top of his salary. It seemed to make sense to buy Roger something 'tasty'; if it meant boosting his chances, then a decent bottle of scotch was a small price to pay.

John preferred not to go to the canteen at lunchtime, but occasionally, for the sake of keeping in with his colleagues, he made a concession. While feeling irked that he still had at least half a thermos flask full, he would drink a cup of tepid liquid the colour of boot polish and attempt to join in the conversation. The dreaded Christmas party was about all anyone talked about.

'Blimey, that little Tricia from accounts was a goer last year, wasn't she?' someone said with a chorus of agreement. John tried to look interested, although hearing she had performed a striptease right down to her undies seemed unlikely. Perhaps they were over-egging things to make him say something foolish. He was still trying to work out this line of banter that nearly always involved alcohol and a female doing something untoward.

Roger dug him in the ribs. 'This is why we don't allow wives to come, they'd spoil all the fun, eh?'

'I should say they would,' murmured John, feeling relieved that at least the line between work and home had a clear divide.

◦◦◦◦◦

An office party was a nightmarish combination of small talk, fancy food, popular music, dancing and overindulging in alcohol. In summary, it amounted to people losing control to the point that they became next year's office gossip. It was bad enough that John had to spend all day with the group of men he was supposed to see as colleagues, let alone waste an evening with them. Still, he'd handed over ten shillings and had no choice about going, so he would just stay long enough to show his face and be seen by the bosses.

'I won't be late. Back by nine-thirty. Ten at the latest,' he told Flora on the last Friday before Christmas.

He pretended not to hear her saying, 'It's a shame I can't come with you,' and focused on adjusting his tie in the hall mirror before shrugging on his overcoat. If he hurried, he could catch the seven-fifteen and get the whole sorry business over and done with, sooner rather than later.

The canteen had been transformed into a passable party venue with festooning paper chains and clusters of balloons. The

Formica topped tables, now covered with red cloths, were arranged at jaunty angles around the edge of the room. A long buffet table and a makeshift bar were at the back of the room and a stage at the front. John eyed the expanse of open flooring in the middle with a sense of foreboding. Hopefully, it was only for dancing, which he wouldn't be doing in any case, rather than ridiculous party games someone had mentioned. He'd have more difficulty getting out of those, unless he managed to leave before they got started.

He looked around for anyone he should go and talk to. As a new recruit, there weren't many people he knew that well; there were whole departments at Franklin Union he had nothing to do with. Perhaps he'd better get a drink. May as well get his money's worth; at least they had Double Diamond on draft.

'Excuse me,' said John, trying to attract the barman's attention. Everyone was making the most of the 'free' drinks. Susie and Pamela were in front of him ordering port and lemon. He could try and squeeze in next to them.

'Look who's here, Pammie,' Susie said, then winked at John and added, 'Don't forget to ask me for a dance, Mr Marshall, I bet you're a proper little raver.'

'See you later,' said Pamela with a smile and followed Susie, who was saying something about finding a seat, right in the middle of the action.

John joined a table of salesmen and tried to recall their names while they discussed the physical attributes of the telephonists sitting across the room.

'Tina's the foxiest chick at Franklin, it's a sin to have her hidden away in the exchange.'

'Yeah, but Maggie's got the legs.'

'Legs are one thing, but which one's going to hand out a portion?'

John checked his watch, nodded and smiled when necessary, and breathed a sigh of relief when, finally, the buffet was opened.

He'd have his food, wait 'til the dancing started and then slope off. With any luck he'd be home by nine.

As soon as the meal was over and the tables cleared away, Roger jumped on the stage, grabbed a microphone and went through the process of saying 'one-two, one-two. Testing, one-two, one-two,' until someone shouted, 'Get on with it.'

'That was a lovely spread, put on by our very own Shirley and Betty from the canteen, let's give them a round of applause.'

John clapped enthusiastically, having made three trips to the buffet table to get his money's worth. He would have stuck to sandwiches, hard-boiled eggs and cheese straws, but on the last trip there wasn't any proper food left so he put a vol-au-vent on his plate, and it was actually quite nice. After each visit to the buffet, he passed the bar and awarded himself another beer. By his calculation, he had used up two-thirds of his ten shillings ticket, based on commercial prices. He only needed to drink three more pints to break even.

'Now then ladies and gents, how about a bit of friendly competition? Thanks to Senior Management, we have a veritable treasure trove of prizes, and seeing as Franklin Union have just had their best year ever, I think that's only right and proper we share out the spoils.' An enthusiastic cheer rippled around the room.

'Let's have the grafters up here. You know who I'm talking about. No, not you, George, I said grafters. The backbone of the company. Our very own brilliant sales negotiators. Come on gents, without you we wouldn't have customers, come on up. That's it, stand in a row and let's show them who you are.'

John had followed his colleagues in front of the stage and faced the crowded tables, smiling sheepishly while everyone clapped. He'd never felt so appreciated. What a marvellous evening.

'Righty-ho. Now, where would we be without our talented typists, our telephone operators, or our two glamorous receptionists? Come on up girls, don't be shy.'

With much more enthusiastic applause, cheers and several wolf-whistles, almost all the women in the room filed up, laughing and waving at the remainder of the audience. After a few comments from Roger along the lines of 'Phwoar! Get a load of our Franklin beauties,' and 'Give us a twirl, girls.' John hoped that would be it, and they could all sit down again; after all that beer, he could do with going to the lavatory

Roger was telling them to mix up and form four lines of male, female, male, female. What was going on? John found himself wedged between Pamela and a typist called Coleen who had a reputation for setting the eighty-seven words-per-minute office record. While he had every respect for her professional capacity, he had never even spoken to her before and it seemed to him she was standing rather too close. But before he could decide if he should shake hands with Coleen and maybe congratulate her on her typing speed, she had turned to his male counterpart on her other side and seemed to be doing something inappropriate. Not kissing exactly but…

Hang on! The other teams were all doing it as well. Oh no. What hellish thing is this? Pass the sodding orange. He'd sooner pay another ten shillings than extract citrus fruit from under the chin of a barely acquainted female. And then, worse, pass it on to Pamela.

Pamela.

Pamela with the glossy brown hair.

Pamela with the letterbox red lips.

Pamela with a cleavage to rival the Paps of Jura.

CHAPTER 17

FLORA

Flora hadn't spoken to her parents since the morning of her wedding, and even then, it hadn't been a conversation, just Dad shouting through the bathroom door while she got ready. Christmas was the perfect time to try and patch things up. Catching a bus home felt strange. She sat on the top deck on the righthand side, so that when they passed Fine Fare she could look down at the shop front, maybe even see a familiar face. They'd changed the way they used to do the window display. A year ago, she had been in charge of Christmas. She'd made a good job of it, always making sure everything was topped up, displaying the more expensive tins of biscuits at jaunty angles. A couple of days before Christmas Eve, when she'd piled all the remaining stock in the window with 'Last Minute Treats' written in red pen underneath, everything had sold out. Perhaps that was her finest hour?

A lot of things had changed in a year.

She began to feel sick. Nerves. What if Mum and Dad told her to go away? What if they didn't even open the door? She wouldn't stay long, just have a quick cup of tea and say, 'Happy Christmas', then maybe sometime after New Year, they could come over for Sunday lunch and get to know John.

The bus route passed the front gates of St Margaret's but she felt little in the way of nostalgia. The days of hitching her gymslip into her knickers for a game of netball seemed like a different age, and as for Jonny M, well… compared to the John she knew now, he may as well have never existed. She pushed aside the mental replay of John's return from the Christmas party. That was a whole other side to John she didn't want to think about.

When it was time to get off the bus, Flora hesitated. Was she making a mistake? The last Saturday before Christmas was her only chance to be sure Dad was at home, not working and not playing golf. It had always been his day to do odd jobs around the house, put up the tree and climb a step ladder to arrange the paper chains however Mum wanted them. She hadn't told John she was going, and she hadn't telephoned her parents to say she was coming. It wouldn't matter if she changed her mind.

'Come on, Missy. On or off?' The bus driver was waiting.

Someone standing behind her tried to get past and bumped her on the back of her legs with a bag of shopping. She stepped down onto the pavement and moved aside to let the other passengers off. Perhaps she'd just walk down their road, past the house, just to see how she felt.

It was only three o'clock in the afternoon, but the Christmas tree lights were already on. It was set up in the usual spot, decorated with familiar coloured baubles, exactly as it had been last year and for every year she could remember. But it had always been her job to switch the lights on at five o'clock. Having them on in broad daylight wasn't something she ever remembered happening. She opened the front gate and went to the window. The side table had been cleared of ornaments and instead, there were plates of food. Party food. Cheese and pineapple on sticks, Twiglets, vol-au-vents. Her mother came in carrying a plate of devilled eggs. She had her party makeup on, which was more than her shopping makeup and many lipsticks beyond her at-home makeup. Seeing her hair still in curlers while putting the food out meant there was probably about half an hour to go before guests arrived. She stepped back from the window, trying to decide if she should go in and whether to knock first or just walk in as though it was still her home.

Muffled voices. Dad was there. A quick look confirmed it; he was wearing a cravat and a new corduroy jacket that somehow made him look younger. Dashing, even. Flora watched him pour Mum a glass of sherry. They looked happy. Celebrating as though their only child leaving home was a good reason to have a party. Well, good riddance. She'd always known her mother hadn't wanted children but she thought Dad could have looked less cheerful. Clearly, he was managing perfectly well without his 'Pickle'. She quietly closed the garden gate behind her and hurried back towards the bus stop with her head down, not wishing to be seen by anyone.

On her way back to Grove Road, Flora mulled over the situation. She had gone to see her parents on the pretext of saying 'Happy Christmas', but, in fact, wanted to find out if moving back home would be an option, even if it were just for a night. If she had somewhere else to go, she wouldn't have considered asking them. They were her last and only resort. Now she was glad she hadn't knocked on the front door. How smug and happy they were without her. Just seeing them like that made her want to make a success of what they had called 'The biggest mistake of her life'. Even if they were right.

The thought of going back to John was almost enough to make her cry. What had gone wrong? And where was the man she thought she was marrying? She pictured John's sweating, blotchy-red face from the night before. His steamed up glasses, his top button undone and his tie yanked to one side, like a scruffy schoolboy's. The fact he struggled to get his key in the lock at two o'clock in the morning was one thing, but to see him arrive in a taxi had been particularly irksome. She'd never been in a taxi, not even on her wedding day.

She eventually had to open the front door. John fell into the hallway, almost knocking her over as he swan-dived past her.

'Who put that step there?' he said, only it sounded more like, '*hoo-push-shat-shtep-ere*'.

He pulled himself up with the help of the hall table, leaned against the wall and pointed at her,

'Now, be a good wife and –'

'You said you'd be home by ten at the latest. I've been worried sick, why didn't you find a telephone and let me know?'

'Telephone? Why? You'd still be here.' He peeled himself off the wall and tottered towards the stairs. 'You always are.' He began to scramble up the stairs. 'One thing's for certain, you'll always be here. You're my wife.' At the top he turned while gripping the bannister and declared to an invisible audience, 'I'm a married man and I have a wife.'

By the time Flora had reached the bedroom, John was face down across the bed and snoring, still in his overcoat, with his glasses askew.

Flora had already ticked '*For richer or poorer*' off her marriage vows when John lost his job, but she hadn't expected '*In sickness and in health*' to make itself known quite so soon. Not even four months married and she was having to scrape vomit off the candlewick bedspread and leave it to soak in the bath. Knowing John was drunk was clear for anyone to see, but knowing what to do when he passed out and was sick in his sleep was something else. She'd hardly slept after having to wrestle the bedspread from under his uncooperative body, then pull his overcoat and shoes off in order to get him into bed. Her parents had had parties where they drank too much on occasion, but nothing had prepared her for this.

By eleven o'clock in the morning, John was sitting up in bed with a cold flannel over his head and gingerly sipping a cup of tea. 'I'll not go out today. You'll have to take '*The World's Deepest Chasm*' and '*Elementary Potholing*' back to the library, otherwise there'll be a fine.'

He didn't look at all well, but still…

'So you'll fork out to travel in a taxi all over the place, but you won't pay the library fine?'

'It's a matter of principle. Someone else may well wish to withdraw –'

'I don't care about the bloody books! Where were you 'til two – '

John held his finger up. 'I'll thank you for not using foul language, Flora. You'd better hurry if you're going to get there before lunchtime closing.' With that, he lay down and turned his back to her.

Flora had been glad to get out of the house. She had returned the books and carried on to the city centre for some window shopping. She initially only planned to stay out until after lunchtime and see how he liked being the one left waiting. As time went on, she felt less and less inclined to go home, so she caught the bus that would take her past Fine Fare and on to her parent's house.

It had been a spur of the moment decision to go, and now she'd been, she knew leaving John wasn't an option, at least not in the immediate future. Travelling back to Grove Road, Flora concluded that at least she had been missing for several hours and hopefully, he would be frantic with worry, wondering where *she* was for a change.

CHAPTER 18

JOHN

Akin to the devastating liquefaction following the 1964 Niigata earthquake, the taxi-vomit-stay-in-bed episode left John's position as head of the household on shaky ground. Flora had dutifully cleaned up his mess, combed sick out of his hair and washed his glasses in carbolic soap. She had returned his library books but then stayed out for most of the day. When she'd come home, she'd cooked their evening meal and eaten her faggots and peas in silence. He'd been grateful for the lack of conversation; just the smell of hot gravy had almost brought on another bout of retching. He had left his plate untouched and gone back to bed while Flora spent a second night on the sofa.

By Sunday evening she was almost back to normal and wanted to discuss their Christmas dinner menu. From then on, she seemed focused on the forthcoming festivities. With the domestic situation more or less under control, John was left to wrestle with his conscience whenever the occasional flashback from the office Christmas party caught him unawares. Something to do with Pamela and a bottle of crème de menthe. And for some reason, the thought of cherry brandy turned his stomach. Dancing? He couldn't imagine how that had come about. He didn't want to. Still, Flora knew none of that, so all he needed to do was bide his time, carry on as normal, and his authority as husband and householder would be fully restored.

A final week at work should see everything back on an even keel by Christmas. On Monday morning, an accident involving a milk float and a lorry load of vegetables meant John only just arrived at Franklin's on time. He had planned to be at the office even earlier than his usual half-hour, and be settled at his desk, already engrossed in something to avoid the inevitable post-party banter. No matter, by walking in at just before nine o'clock, his colleagues should have finished dissecting the merits of Betty's legs and Moira's breasts or whatever else had happened. All he had to do was get past Roger's office.

'Well, well, they say it's the quiet ones,' he said with a smirk.

'I don't think I –' Despite the most awful hangover, only comparable to a time at university when someone's homemade parsnip wine had rendered him speechless for two days, he was fairly sure nothing of any significance had happened. Apart from perhaps a bit of dancing. With Pamela. While swigging a bit of Crème de Menthe. Straight from the bottle.

'Don't worry, we're all one big family here. No need for apologies, we all get a bit carried away now and then.'

'Well, I don't think there's much to apologise for.' Or was there? Had he really bent Pamela over a table and patted her bottom in time to the music? No, surely not. She'd given him a cheery smile when he arrived that morning, so no harm there.

'I must say, I've never seen anything quite like it, but at least the lads were entertained. Maybe next year we'll get you up on the stage for a full show.'

'I don't think that's necessary.'

Roger slapped John on the back as he sidled past, then called after him, 'That's right mate, deny all knowledge. I would.'

That should be the worst of it. Hopefully, everyone in the sales office would be cracking on with their leads, keen to close any last sales and gain their full Christmas bonus.

'Whhhey-heyy! Here he is, the boy wonder.'

'How do you do it, eh?'

'He's a dark horse.'

John smiled weakly. If only he could recall the facts, perhaps he could come up with something to say, he was sure there'd been nothing more than a couple of dances with Pamela. If they were entertained by his lack of prowess on the dance floor, so be it. He thought he'd made rather a good job of it, considering the frantic rhythm of popular music and the hindrance of his dodgy leg.

CHAPTER 19

FLORA

As Christmas Day approached, Flora consulted Mrs Beeton; when it came to special occasions, she and Mrs B were on the same page. Her sumptuous five-course dinners were an inspiration, especially the way she topped them off with a selection of celebration jellies; magnificent structures of glorious wobbliness decorated with piped cream and strategically placed crystallised fruit. Undoubtedly Mrs B could make a meal of every occasion. She even had several pages dedicated to folding serviettes. Should she go for Fleur de Lis, Cockscomb or The Vase? Flora had practised them all using sheets of old newspaper until she settled on the elegant yet simple Rose.

In *'Christmas dinner with the middle classes of this empire'*, Mrs Beeton conjures up a cosy image of carving a fat turkey, saying she *'can hardly imagine an object of greater envy'*. Mum had always roasted a turkey too, then invited friends and neighbours for a Boxing Day buffet to help use up the leftovers. As it would just be the two of them, she would make do with a family-sized chicken and fill it with Mrs Beeton's *'hearty and rich festive stuffing'*, but maybe leaving out the goose liver and prunes.

On Christmas morning, Flora got up early to prepare their special lunch. She would have liked a prawn cocktail to start but John said he wouldn't eat aquatic crustaceans and opted for oxtail soup instead. No matter, she had bought a couple of fancy bread rolls to have on the side and, thanks to Mrs B's handy tip, had learned to make pretty curls of butter using a wet serrated knife. A roast chicken with bread sauce and all the trimmings would follow. And then the main event. A wonderfully boozy sherry trifle made with a home-baked sponge base, soaked in their wedding day Bristol Cream. Flora added almost a whole jar of raspberry jam, a pint each of custard and whipped cream, topped off with a festive design of glacé cherries and pretend holly leaves cut out of angelica.

Flora checked the chicken was cooked through and put the plates to warm. She laid the table with the addition of red paper napkins, already folded into roses from the day before. For extra Christmas cheer, she dipped the dampened rim of each wine glass in sugar to make them look frosty. With a bottle of chilled Lambrusco open, ready to be poured and everything timed to perfection, she took off her apron and nipped upstairs to get change. She could just about squeeze into the same outfit she'd worn last Christmas; Dad had said she looked lovely in her red long-sleeved mini and white go-go boots, very Christmassy.

Party makeup was a must. Three coats of black mascara and a generous application of Winter Frost eyeshadow was a step in the right direction, but Tangerine Dream lipstick transformed her into the hot-blooded woman she had been on her wedding day. She practised a Bridgette Bardot style 'Happy Christmas, darling,' and pictured John's delight when he realised what a Christmas cracker he had for a wife. She imagined him giving her the necklace she'd been dropping hints about and kissing her neck as he stood behind her to fasten it. 'You're so beautiful,' he'd murmur and with a further embrace, all the unpleasantness of the previous weekend would be forgotten.

Back downstairs, she waited outside the sitting room door to savour the moment before making her entrance. John was standing over the stereo, about to give Jim Reeves a turn on the player.

He stared at her with the record frozen in mid-air. 'What on earth have you done to yourself?'

'I thought –'

He smiled at Jim Reeves as though sharing a joke and said, '*Little dabs of powder, little pots of paint, makes a girl's complexion, something that it ain't.*' And Jim, who seemed equally pleased with his Twelve Songs of Christmas, smiled back.

Flora ran back upstairs, wept quietly in the bathroom for a few moments and then wiped off her makeup. She blew her nose and splashed her face with cold water to subdue the pinkness. She took a deep breath and looked at herself in the mirror until her reflection was convincing.

John was humming along to Blue Christmas when she returned.

'Here you are, Flora love, Happy Christmas!' he said, handing her a small, neatly wrapped parcel in the shape of a book. When she realised it wasn't the necklace she'd been hoping for, a few more tears trickled the remains of mascara down her face.

'Come on, now,' said John, taking her by the shoulders. 'You know I love you just the way you are.'

'Yes,' she said.

'All the way to the Congo and back,' he added. And that was one of the very few times he had mentioned love since they had been married, so she knew she'd done the right thing by wiping her face clean

CHAPTER 20

JOHN

Christmas had passed pleasantly enough, despite a slight altercation before lunch, when Flora had slathered herself in cosmetics. The rest of the day had been almost the same as when Mother was alive. John was surprised to realise his wife was by far the superior cook. Even thinking such a thing felt like a betrayal, but in the end he felt a small compliment was in order and said, 'Goodness me, that Christmas dinner was as good as Mothers, if not a touch better.'

His gift of '*The History of Domestic Appliances*' in hardback seemed to go down well and although he wouldn't be wearing the cravat Flora had given him, it had been nice to have a parcel to open. The Queen's Christmas Broadcast was as excellent as always, with Her Majesty's recollection of the year's travel, accompanied by footage of her visits to Canada, Australia and New Zealand. The speech gave him the idea of getting out his copy of the world map to entertain Flora and identify all the places in the Commonwealth.

The impromptu geography lesson filled up the gap until tea time, when Flora brought out a Christmas cake, iced with what she described as snowy peaks. The regularly spaced points of icing over the entire cake were child-like, but so as not to spoil the day, he managed to hold back from saying it was unrealistic to have a snow formation without undulation or drift. Instead, he used the opportunity to discuss the multiplicity of Eskimo words for snow, taking into account the polysynthetic nature of the Inuit language.

Filling the gulf of time between Christmas and New Year had been a challenge. There was nothing to do at the allotment, although before visiting Mother's grave with a holly wreath, his sense of duty compelled him to pop in to check on 'The Girls'. Without their summer foliage, their tubers were now dusted with yellow sulphur, wrapped in newspaper and stored in the potting shed.

The library was only open for three days, then closed until after the New Year. He would have gone to work if he'd been able, but Franklin Union Insurance was also closed for business until the first working week of 1971. While Flora did her housework he sat in the sitting room and read the newspaper, but as soon as she'd finished and a possible conversation would be pending, or worse, the suggestion of a walk, he felt the need to make himself scarce.

He spent much of each day hiding in what Flora referred to as the spare room. It was Mother's room. And as it still housed her things along with his growing collection of National Geographic, there was nothing 'spare' about it. The holiday period was the perfect time to re-catalogue the back issues into his own classification system. Qualifying each magazine he assessed the most interesting feature as a primary category and then based a sub-category on the geographical location of such features. This took some time, given the conundrum of multiple articles of interest and diverse locations within each publication. Some articles were so fascinating that he had to stop work and re-read them, then had an internal debate on the merits of which stand out feature should indicate the lead category.

Until the sort out, his National Geographics had been stacked on the bedroom floor and assimilated an alpine range, modified by glacial erosion where a steep incline was required to provide access to Mother's dressing table. But now, *'First Explorers on the Moon - the Story of Apollo 11'* required a stand-alone category and *'global weather phenomenon'* needed a whole new section; it was necessary for magazines to flow across Mother's bed, submerging her pink candlewick in a sea of yellow rectangles.

Besides the library's closure, the other irritation during the Christmas holidays was Flora's insatiable sexual appetite. While he had been using the excuse of working late and tiredness to avoid the act, he had nowhere to hide when there was little else to do but read in the evenings. Watching rubbish on television until the last program at eleven-thirty was the worst decoy as Flora simply stayed up then followed him to bed. Although sexual intercourse provided a mildly enjoyable sensation, he would rather not. So far as he was concerned, the marriage had already been consummated; he wasn't required to do any more than that, but for the sake of peace, he relented on no fewer than two occasions.

⚬⚬⚬

With Christmas out of the way and no need for further fuss or frivolities for the next few months, John was determined to concentrate on his career. He had hardly had time to put his training into practice before they had closed for Christmas. He planned to start the New Year with a bang, and make 1971 the beginning of his success in insurance sales. The annual targets had already been set and he was determined to be one of the few who earned at least one of the much-coveted Monthly Bonanza prizes. The prizes were kept secret until someone won them and could be anything from a new briefcase to a bicycle. Whatever it was, it was worth having on top of his basic salary and commission. Being a Bonanza recipient would also stand him in good stead when the call of promotion beckoned.

Working late at the office had many advantages, primarily by telephoning households at that time enabled him to speak to the man of the house, who would be home from work by then. Being able to speak directly with the decision-maker often meant closing the sale there and then. A warm-up conversation on the telephone with a wife during the day could be helpful, but firming-up the agreement and the all important signature required the husband. Often this meant one of the field sales team calling at the property with an appointment, but then the commission had to be split. John would much rather try do the whole thing himself on the telephone and send the documents in the post.

Most of the sales team chose to leave between five and five-thirty. After that, it was just John in the salesroom and sometimes Roger in his office next door. Roger made no bones about it; he liked to stay away from home until his children were in bed, which meant hanging around until opening time at The Red Lion at six o'clock. Thereafter, John was his own man.

Despite interrupting evening meals across Coventry, he knew that with persistence, enough calls would guarantee a sale. The eighty-twenty rule was simple macroeconomics, and when combined with a thick skin and an eye on the prize, he was destined to become Salesman of The Year. To make it more fun, he developed a little chart to prove the eighty-twenty rule was working and to keep a note of the most common rejections. It also showed an interesting pattern in his progress: 'Bugger off 'and 'Not you again 'were the most frequent, however, 'Blood-sucking nuisance 'or simply having the line disconnect almost disappeared after a few weeks, when his telephone technique became more polished.

The results were encouraging, but while John concentrated on disturbing households far and wide with talk of death, destitute widows and the marvellous solution that was Franklin Union Insurance, he failed to realise that someone was watching and waiting.

And by the time he did, it was too late.

Whatever Pamela thought he had intended at the Christmas party was simply not the case, but she had taken it into her head that his working late at the office had something to do with her. Some sort of elaborate excuse for them to be more intimate. If only he could remember the full facts, then he might be able to reason with her. Instead, he had to fend off what he could only assume were romantic advances. A cup of tea brought to his desk after hours, the offer to help with his paperwork. The suggestion of a nightcap back at her place. Absurd to think he'd gone through his life without the slightest interest from the fairer sex, and just like that, they were all over him like flies.

CHAPTER 21

FLORA

After that first Christmas, whenever Flora felt a bit miserable, she'd dress up and put on her Tangerine Dream lipstick. She wouldn't be wearing it for John anymore, but there was no reason why she shouldn't wear it for herself. As with many aspects of her marriage, she was learning of ways to make the most of her mundane tasks. Instead of following John's list of instructions to buy bread from one shop and bacon from another, as his Mother had done, Flora opted for a supermarket. The convenience was one thing but the cheaper prices meant there was always a small surplus in her housekeeping allowance, enough for a frothy coffee and maybe even an iced bun. Gail's Cafe was her favourite. With pretty gingham tablecloths and friendly staff, a couple of short conversations with a cheerful waitress was enough to keep her going for the rest of the week. She was always home in time to remove her makeup, change back into her 'usual' clothes and have the evening meal well on the way before she heard John's key in the door.

Another benefit of shopping at a supermarket was Green Shield Stamps. John had been saving stamps for years and as part of his Saturday routine, would lick and stick them into an orange book. He had amassed a small pile of books and kept them stashed in the bottom of the wardrobe, saying they would buy a new television when the time came. But even at a glance, Flora could see they were a long way off eighty-eight books for a Regentone 19" television or even thirty-two books for a Kenwood Chef. John had written '*Remember GST (Green Shield Stamps)*' next to the weekly shopping list with a corresponding asterisk next to *Patels Corner Shop and J.O. Davies, Greengrocer* on the housework rota. Neither the butcher or the baker offered stamps, but the supermarket did. Sometimes they even had Double Stamp Days.

Flora stuck the excess stamps in her secret book and stashed it in a tin behind the ironing board. With enough books, she could treat herself to a hairdryer or even a set of Carmen Heated Rollers. The tin was fast becoming a little treasure trove of goodies: there was always a packet of emergency Jelly Babies and at least one packet of biscuits. Lemon Puffs or Tunnock's Teacakes with a nice cup of tea never failed whenever she needed a pick-me-up.

Flora went shopping at least two, sometimes three times a week, depending on the housework rota. '*Dust all skirting boards and vacuum hall, stairs and landing*' was hardly a chore. If she only did the bits that needed it she could be heading for the bus stop by ten o'clock, and with a sandwich in her handbag, she could make a day of it. After wandering around Woolworths, she would head to C&A where she could try a few things on without feeling the pressure to buy. Then on to Golden Discs to have a go with Cliff Richard in a listening booth. After finding a quiet spot to have her lunchtime sandwich, she'd head to the supermarket and tick a few things off John's list, then call in at Gail's Cafe on the way back to the bus stop.

If she chose the right seat on the bus ride home, she could have a nice chat about the weather with a friendly housewife, then better than the conversation itself, a cheerful 'cheerio' at the end, as though they were more than strangers. She was almost making friends and sometimes, not often, she would see the same person twice so the conversation could advance to something a little more meaningful.

'Hello, how are you?' She had sat next to the same elderly lady a couple of weeks before and heard how, despite her arthritis, she had knitted all her grandchildren a pair of mittens for Christmas. Sixteen pairs. Blue for the boys and pink for the girls.

'Oh, hello, deary, I'm well enough thank you, how's yourself?' She shuffled over to make room for Flora and her shopping.

'I'm very well, thank you,'

'You know how much I spent on m'bread and whatnot this week? With that new money, 'parently, we don't get two hundred and forty pennies in the pound no more, only a hundred. Daylight robbery!'

'It's confusing, isn't it?' She had only just worked things out herself, John had spent a considerable amount of time, totting up the housekeeping in new money and decided on three pounds, which was quite a leap from one pound, fifteen shillings and sixpence. Flora was thrilled until she did a week's worth of shopping and had to ask him for another twenty-two new pence to pay the milkman.

'That decimal currency's a scandal.' The old lady took out a handkerchief and blew her nose. 'I've a shocking cold and now I'm stuck for brandy. Medicinal you understand. Have to wait 'til next pension I s'pect.'

By the time the old lady stood up to leave, Flora had heard all about her children living too far away to visit and the trouble she'd had getting the top off a jar of marmalade.

'Perhaps I can help,' she blurted out. 'I'm Flora by the way, I live in Grove Road. Next stop.'

'Well, if you wouldn't mind calling by some time, deary, I've a couple of things need doing and I don't like my neighbours. Noisy blighters. Upstairs and down. I'm in the flats on Elizabeth Street, number seven. Peggy Chance.'

'Alright Peggy, how about tomorrow at two o'clock?'

Flora walked home feeling she had finally made a breakthrough. Even a grumpy old grandmother could be a friend. She already knew she wouldn't tell John; she needed something of her own. Another thing.

~~~

Peggy had lived through two world wars, had three husbands, six children and sixteen grandchildren. She'd been a chorus girl in the first world war and a hostel warden for a munitions factory in the second; she would have preferred to entertain the troops again but by then she had birthed six babies and didn't have the legs.

Flora was transfixed by her stories and poured her another glass of Bristol Cream. She'd take the bottle back home and top it up with something cheaper before next Christmas, John would never know.

'I've seen my share of death, and not just in wartime. Two children. Three husbands.' Peggy chatted almost non-stop for two hours with tales of how she had crossed the English Channel at night in boats loaded with goods for the army.

'All us girls, squeezed together, sitting on sacks of spuds from Newhaven.'

'Gosh. You were in a dance troupe heading into enemy lines under the cover of darkness? How romantic.'

'We'd do a show for the troops, head back the same night. Oftentimes we'd have a few wounded soldiers on board. We'd try and cheer 'em up. Light them a ciggy, have a chat.' Flora held her breath while Peggy took a swig of Bristol Cream. 'Met my Alfie that way. Married as soon as he was fit, lost on the Eastern Front. Widowed at nineteen with a baby on the way.'

Flora cried at this, partly for the tragedy, but also with the realisation that Peggy had already known romance, excitement and travel before she was twenty. How did that compare to shelf

122

stacking at Fine Fare and never been abroad, apart from Wales. And now she was married to the most unromantic man in the world, was that it?

A weekly visit to Peggy's flat became a welcome addition to Flora's routine. Armed with a bottle of whatever was on offer at the supermarket, Peggy was always ready with the kettle on and a string of stories to tell. Time seemed to fly by, so when a brisk walk home had to become an ungainly gallop, Flora took John's bedside alarm clock in her handbag and set it for quarter-past four, knowing it would take at least another fifteen minutes to have 'one last cuppa' before extracting herself from Peggy's world.

The old lady was even more lonely than Flora and had a knack for keeping her audience right where she wanted; sitting on her late husband's recliner with a milky cup of tea and an arrowroot biscuit. As a seasoned entertainer, she reeled off almost unbelievable stories: a virgin pregnancy, the cure for a broken heart or the aristocratic lady with an insatiable love of gambling. Each visit provided Flora with a new perspective on life she'd barely thought of before. And when it came to John and his penny-pinching ways, Peggy had first-hand experience, having had a short-lived fling with a miser, who counted the lumps of coal she put on the fire and watered down the milk to make it go further.

~∽૭૭∽~

Despite John's promise made during their honeymoon-week-at-home, to make their house 'a little paradise', nothing more than Flora's attempt to paint the kitchen, and a few emergency repairs had been done. Most of the decor had been carried out in the late forties by his mother. The yellowing walls were punctuated here and there by small rectangles of colour where hanging pictures had preserved the original wallpaper. The bathroom lino was so worn that the pattern in front of the sink had disappeared altogether, as though losing the will to live.

On Peggy's advice, a trip to Laura Ashley was in order; now that John had a steady job, it was time for him to honour his promise. Flora spent an enjoyable hour in the shop, comparing a dizzying array of floral patterned wallpaper and curtain fabric with corresponding paint and cushion covers. Back in the cave-like sitting room at Grove Road, she laid out the snipped samples of fabric and a few paint charts on the coffee table and repeated the sales spiel to John, particularly that it would add value to the property, should they decide to sell. 'Laura Ashley is very happening, very now,' she added.

John's silence spoke volumes.

'It's what everyone wants,' she trailed off.

'This matchy-matchy business is women's nonsense. And as we'll not be moving house, give me one good reason why it serves us better than what we already have?' He picked his newspaper back up, indicating the matter was closed and left Flora trying to think of something more to say. He always had to have the last word. It wasn't worth trying to reason with him when it came to spending money.

She now had a coping strategy, guaranteed to make herself feel better, albeit silently. The story behind the advice was due to Peggy's husband number three, who she had married out of fear of being alone after George, her second and most beloved husband, died in a freak accident. The man turned out to be a bully who wouldn't stand for anyone else to have the last word, and if they did he ended matters once and for all with his fists. According to Peggy, every woman should develop a few special ways, 'To keep afloat'.

In the redecorating conversation or the lack of it, Flora felt inclined to go straight upstairs and exact her silent last word. While John continued to read about '*Thatcher The Milk Snatcher*' and BOAC's 747 maiden flight, she took his toothbrush and scrubbed it around the inside rim of the lavatory. Then, she offered to make him a cup of tea and served it with a smile and a

Garibaldi biscuit. Later, while John watched Horizon, she had a pang of guilt and went back upstairs to rinse the worst of the germs off under the cold tap.

Whenever hurt feelings or disillusion inevitably distilled into anger, Flora employed her new coping strategy by sprinkling salt on John's portion of jam roly-poly or moving the buttons further apart on his work shirt. Not having a promised new pair of shoes for a birthday present or being told she was a blithering idiot became a lot less upsetting when she watched John's nose twitch, possibly detecting a sardine tang on his Garibaldi. Then once a week, along with a tot or two of sherry to ease Peggy's lumbago, chilblains or whatever the mythical ailment might be, Flora re-told the scene with a few embellishments and by the time they had finished laughing, she almost felt sorry for him.

༼ঌৡ঩༽

As Flora's first wedding anniversary came into view, a marital rhythm had been established. In the Marshall household, there were no surprises or arguments, no strangers at the door or foreign foods on the table. Flora had learnt that when John was out of the house, small freedoms made her life worth living. She could switch on the radio at full blast and dance around the kitchen, raid the treat box hidden behind the ironing board, or sit and soothe herself with a daily soap opera and bask in the reassurance that other people's problems were far worse than hers.

With the summer of 1971 already upon them, it seemed more than a year since she'd left Fine Fare with dreams of a great adventure, romance and sophisticated dinner parties. It hadn't started off like that with John's job loss and she still hadn't done any of the things she'd imagined a new wife would. Not redecorated the house or installed a doorbell. No dinner parties or coffee mornings. And only Peggy for a new friend. No matter, she was still young. All sorts of things could happen; if John kept going with his overtime, he might even become a manager. Then they would have children and move to a nice house with a proper garden. A new home would feel more like hers. And who knew what else was in store.

She was only nineteen years old. There was a chance John would change, maybe when they had children he'd lighten up a bit more. And in the back of her mind was the fact Peggy had had three husbands. The possibility of another marriage somewhere down the line wasn't out of the question. Nothing was forever.

Meanwhile, their first wedding anniversary was coming up. Although Mrs Beeton didn't seem to celebrate such occasions, Flora was planning a candlelit dinner for two with swan folded serviettes and flowers on the table. Despite John's protestations, she also insisted they buy each other an anniversary present. 'It doesn't have to be expensive. It's the thought that counts.'

She had seen a lovely paisley tie in Foster Brothers, orange, yellow and brown, so almost the sort of colours John liked, but groovy. She went back to look at it several times. How could she make John more 'with it' without him noticing? Peggy said it was possible, bit by bit. Perhaps paisleys were too much of a leap. In the end, she bought something closer to the one he always wore, still brown, but with a small repeat burgundy and cream motif. Subtle. That would be the start of remodelling John into a man of the future.

She wrapped the tie in a reused piece of least Christmassy-looking Christmas paper. And tied a bow around it using a strip of fabric cut from the bottom of her high-waister trousers, which were now too small. She twirled some more of the material around a household candle, set it on a saucer in the middle of the table and picked an overhanging sunflower from next door's garden. John had been threatening to cut it off for trespassing in any case. The most exciting thing on the table, however, was a bottle of Mateus Rose. She had seen it advertised on television, it simply shouted romantic, exotic, faraway places. Yes, it was expensive, but with all the overtime John must be earning, he couldn't refuse an anniversary treat, and next year she could use the oval-shaped empty bottle as a candlestick holder.

For an added romantic ambience, she had wrestled the kitchen table into the sitting room and covered it with a cloth. She had half thought of cleaning out what had once been a dining room, but it was full of John's mothers' things, including an old sewing machine and John's childhood bed, dismantled and propped up against the heavy set dining table.

Her adaptation of a 'John safe' chicken supreme recipe with the garlic, cream and mustard purposefully left out, was keeping warm in the oven, and everything else was ready. Flora took her hair out of its ponytail and brushed it. That would do in terms of getting ready; she knew there was no point in getting dressed up, and in any case, she didn't have that much choice, now she'd grown out of all her fashionable stuff.

She settled down to await John's return from work and watched television over the top of the temporary dining table that almost blocked the screen. One of the good things about John working longer hours meant she could watch an entire episode of Crossroads before he got home, instead of having to switch Meg Mortimer off in mid-crisis and then try and piece things together during the next episode.

The sound of a key in the door at half-past six was a relief. Flora quickly lit the candle, then hurried to the hall to usher John to the table.

'Goodness, you've completely rearranged the place, what's all the fuss about?'

'Pour the wine, John. I'll just sort out our starter.'

'Starter? It's only a first wedding anniversary, hardly worth celebrating.'

She would have liked to have had a fondue; was there anything more romantic for an anniversary than sharing a meal heated over a naked flame? She had tried to assure John it was just a different way of eating a sandwich and that by pronging bread into hot cheese, it was more fun, but he hadn't bothered to hide his disgust. Maybe next year. Even a half grapefruit was pushing him into new territory, she knew that, but it was a risk worth taking.

'Here we are,' said Flora, setting the dish down in front of him.

'My heavens, what have we here?' His hand hovered over the teaspoon, waiting for Flora's answer.

It was tempting to answer with one of John's own abrasive put-downs: 'are you a complete imbecile?' Or 'honestly, your lack of intellect sometimes astounds me'. Instead, she said, 'It's a citrus first course, topped with a glacé cherry. Good for your digestion and full of vitamins.'

'I hope you're not going into all that new-fangled health food nonsense.' He watched Flora spoon her second and third mouthful. 'I'm willing to give most things a try, but this is testing the limit.' He ate a few segments without chewing properly and swigged his wine afterwards.

In the kitchen, Flora finished John's remaining grapefruit and sucked the sugary cherry while she spooned peas and mashed potato onto two plates. She would carry the casserole dish to the table for the extra ceremony and by doing so, hopefully, remind him it was a special occasion. She wished she had made the dish properly now, but with extra garlic, just to teach him a lesson. He really should expand his horizons.

After the main course, which John seemed to enjoy, Flora released two Mrs Beeton inspired individual puddings; mandarins in blancmange jelly. She had used teacups for moulds and was delighted with the resulting wobbly domes. She topped each one with a blob of cream and a mandarin segment. If he didn't want to eat his, Flora would have it. She half hoped he wouldn't, as it would be a nice treat for her elevenses the next day.

With the meal finished, it was time for presents. At least the brown envelope with Flora's name on most definitely wasn't a book. Opening *Thrifty Tips for the Modern Housewife* on her birthday had been a crashing disappointment.

'I wonder what it can be?' A single sheet of card by the feel of it, maybe a love note or a poem? John wasn't very expressive like that, but there was always hope.

'The first anniversary is celebrated with a paper gift. I think you'll find it useful in the future,' said John.

Flora's heart sank. Useful translated into boring. She opened the envelope, already exhaling with resignation and not at all surprised to pull out a metric conversion chart. She already had one pinned up inside a kitchen cabinet; if he ever offered to make a cup of tea, he'd know that. She'd just become used to decimal currency, and now there were going to be litres and kilos, but not yet, thank goodness.

'I just thought you should be prepared, especially if you consider how long it took you to get to grips with the difference between a new five pence piece and an old shilling, remember? You can carry it with you, in your handbag so you can double-check the new weights against the new prices and convert them both back to the old, to double-check.' He took the card and pointed to the top. So, two pounds and two ounces of potatoes will be the same as a new kilogram of potatoes....'

Flora swallowed what would have been a terrifying screech of sheer frustration.

'...And where they were fourpence a pound in old money, you can work out whatever they are in decimal currency and then convert the old weight into grams, which is a fraction of a kilogram, do you see? Learn as you go.'

'Thank you,' was about all she could muster.

Knowing John as well as she did after one year of marriage, he would have spent a considerable amount of time deciding on a paper anniversary present. With her wish not to receive a book, he would have been pushed to come up with anything at all. Would she rather have had another 'useful' book? Perhaps, *Stain Removal for Beginners or The Housewife's Encyclopedia*? Then again, if he marked each passing year with the appropriate gift, would it be worth waiting fifty years to strike gold?

John was undoing her homemade ribbon and being careful not to rip the reused paper.

'My goodness, that's a bit of a bobby-dazzler,' he said without fully removing the tie from the paper, as though once it was released, everything would go out of control.

'Try it on,' insisted Flora. 'It'll make you look younger.'

'You say that as though youth is a good thing,' he said, but was already undoing his plain brown work tie. Then, as they stood side by side in front of the hall mirror, he declared, 'Well, it does have a certain something, without being vulgar or overly obvious. What do you think?'

'You like it?' Finally. Perhaps they were turning a corner.

'I rather think I do, but don't go getting any ideas. I'm not ever going to be one of those snazzy dressers.'

They both laughed at that. And then, when Flora expanded on the idea of him in red velvet bell-bottoms and a mustard coloured polo neck jumper, they laughed some more.

Back at the table, John said, 'Seriously though, I don't think we need to bother with an anniversary present in future, not when we already have each other for life.'

She had to agree. Being married to John was quite enough of a disappointment already.

John topped up their glasses and proposed a toast. 'Here's to the equipotential surfaces of marriage's gravitational field.' He always referred to geography when he was happy.

Flora sipped the pink wine. While enjoying the slight fizz of fruity sunshine on her tongue, she allowed it to transport her to the distant land it had come from. In a mountain vineyard, a handsome peasant picked grapes while dreaming of better times ahead, of the day when he would meet his true love and maybe, just maybe, her name would be Flora.

EPILOGUE

On a February night in 1972, Peggy passed away in her sleep after a short illness. She didn't leave Flora anything in her will, not even the badly painted Staffordshire China dogs, or the malfunctioning cuckoo clock, supposedly carved by a one-armed sailor. Flora could have taken them months ago, when she'd first won them in a game of cards. If she thought about it, she had probably won most of Peggy's personal effects at one time or another. Sometimes twice or three times over. In any case, to suddenly manifest a legacy of ornaments would have taken some explaining to John, who never knew of Peggy, or how she'd taught Flora to cut her own hair, darn socks the old fashioned way and rewire a plug.

On the day of Peggy's funeral, a Thursday, Flora should have cleaned the kitchen and bathroom, done the shopping and prepared toad-in-the-hole for John's evening meal. Instead, she left a tin of spam on the kitchen table with a note saying, *'Doctor's appointment - women's trouble'*, a cast-iron guarantee there would be no questions asked.

In accordance with her old friend's wishes, rather than attend the funeral service, Flora would spend the day at Warwick Castle. Before leaving the house, she checked in her bag for the silver sixpence and turned it over in her hand. It was dated 1921, the year Peggy and 'dear George, my one and only true love,' had married.

A few details had been missing from the plan: almost two hours on the bus for starters and then the pricey entrance fee. No matter, Flora had skimmed the housekeeping money and would find a way to cover her tracks later. All that mattered now was to carry out the deed.

'Fling our lucky sixpence off a tower, into the River Avon,' had sounded so romantic. Dramatic, yet simple. But the idea had not taken into account torrential rain, or that access to the tower might be restricted. Flora would carry out the other instruction first, 'Don't waste money on lunch. Take sandwiches. But treat y'self to a cuppa and a bit of cake.' A slice of coffee and walnut with a pot of tea would go down nicely.

As the rain abated, Flora orientated herself to the river and a suitable vantage point. She took her time to get there by following the arrows through the magnificent banqueting hall and stopped to admire an exhibition of armour. With all the complicated plates, straps and buckles she wondered how on earth Sir Edmond, in *One Hundred Knights*, had managed to swim across a moat in his shining armour, let alone fling it off with a clatter in order to seduce Lady Ellen in her bedchamber.

Sixpence at the ready, Flora looked over the edge of the parapet to the river below. *Something old, something new, something borrowed, something blue and a sixpence in her shoe.* Peggy claimed the happiest day of her life had been on her second wedding day. The war had ended, she and George were in love and years of happiness lay ahead.

'Remember to make a wish, pass on the luck,' the old lady had said when pressing the coin into Flora's hand.

'I will. But why Warwick Castle?'

'Because you'll enjoy the day out.'

Flora kissed the sixpenny piece, made a wish and threw it towards the middle of the river. She didn't see it enter the water. It was gone in an instant.

On the way home, Flora thought about her day with a sense of optimism. She'd never been beyond Coventry on her own, she probably wouldn't go again for some time, but the journey had put something into perspective. She may be married to the meanest, least romantic person in the world, but there would be more to life than just John. Yes, she was a housewife with no money or prospects of her own, but with Peggy as a role model, she knew a life of adventure was yet to come

ACKNOWLEDGEMENTS

For enduring support, friendship and writerly know-how I am forever thankful to a herd of Unicorns, namely, Shivanthi Sathanandan, Julia Lampshire, Anna Davidson, Elizabeth Price, Tamara Henriques, Diane Wilson, David Grievson, David Hayward and Lucy Watkins.

Additionally, many thanks to Alison Taylor, Janette Sullivan, Chandy Rodgers, Clare McVey, Natascha Azevedo, Rachael Workman, Tissie Lilaclicorice for helping to buff my prose.

For hospitality, friendship and compulsory screen breaks, I am grateful to Bertie, Buster and Devon and their lovely owners.

A Note to Readers

If you enjoyed this book, please consider leaving a review. Positive feedback is enormously encouraging for authors, helps their rankings and most of all, by sharing your thoughts, you are helping another reader to make an informed choice.

Please keep in touch

Sign up to receive special offers, bonus content, book promotions or events and updates from the author

www.stellabookchat.com

If you'd like to connect on social media:
Instagram: StellaBookChat
Twitter: @stellabookchat
Facebook: stellabookchat

HOW FLORA FINDS HER FABULOUS
ALSO IN THE FINDING FABULOUS SERIES
Read the first chapter now!

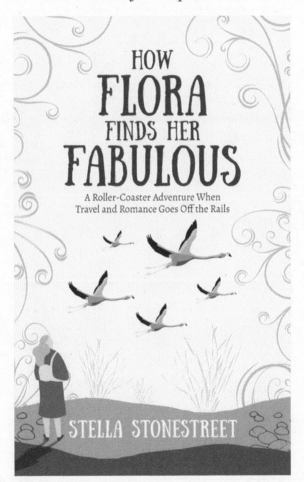

HOW
FLORA
FINDS HER
FABULOUS

A Roller-Coaster Adventure When
Travel and Romance Goes Off the Rails

STELLA STONESTREET

ONE

MONDAY:
Boil egg (4½ mins)
Lay table
Toast (2 slices)
Tea
Prepare packed lunch

In a housewife's champion finish, Flora slapped fish paste onto thin white sliced, clattering and see-sawing the knife's serrated edge on the glass jar. Sounding busy was her speciality. She squashed the sandwiches into an old Stork margarine tub on top of a slice of fruit loaf and jammed the lid on. After pouring tea into a thermos and hurling a banana into John's briefcase, she grabbed a slotted spoon to hook his breakfast out of boiling water. She eyed the kitchen clock with a sense of satisfaction; it had taken years of practice to shave one minute, twelve seconds off his precious schedule.

As usual, John ate his all-too-snotty egg, drank his tea and left for work without a word. The sound of the front door closing heralded a certain calm that left Flora feeling ever-so-slightly lighter. She tuned in to *Wake Up to Wogan* just as Terry was saying 'Did you know cows moo in regional accents?' As on most weekday mornings, he was the first person to speak to her. She hummed along to Bananarama while beating her own breakfast egg, throwing in a wiggle here and there. 'It Ain't What You Do, It's the Way That You Do It'. French toast with sugar sprinkled on top. It was amazing what she could make with John's prescribed breakfast ingredients.

Back in 1970, as a newlywed, she had followed his written instructions to the letter. 'So you don't need to think,' he'd said and, in case she was in any doubt, presented her with *Mrs Beeton's Book of Household Management*, with 'To my wife' inscribed inside. Mrs B was John's second-in-command, unless you counted his long-deceased mother, who still held sway over the decor and furniture.

Over the years, in order to cope with a disappointing husband, she had turned to various sources for advice that was often conflicting and therefore confusing – romantic novels and *Ladies' Circle* versus daytime telly and whatever women's glossy was in the doctor's surgery. Yes, she was her own woman, but thanks to John, Mrs B's bulky authority and old Mother Marshall's ghost, she only truly triumphed during office hours, home alone in the Coventry suburbs.

Moving on to the next of her daily tasks, she wrestled the old twin tub out from under the worktop and forced its hose nozzle onto the kitchen tap. She left the water running and raced upstairs to strip the bed and bring the fully-loaded laundry basket down before the tub was full. She'd only once flooded the kitchen, the day she had stopped to rescue a butterfly trapped in a spider's web.

Coming back down the stairs with a week's worth of washing obscuring her vision was a skill in itself. She concentrated on counting the steps. Terry Wogan was wrapping up his show with a closing pearl of wisdom. 'Don't worry,' he said, 'everybody else thinks they are better looking than they are as well.' Not everybody. She had no illusions about her looks: mousy hair, a few freckles, overweight. It didn't matter anyway. She passed the hall mirror, avoiding eye contact.

First into the machine were her all-too-familiar skirts and blouses, a tangle of American tan tights and a nightie so washed and worn the pink roses were barely discernible. After a ten-minute swish around, she transferred them to the smaller tub for a rinse and spin. The bedding and towels could be washed in one go, but they had to be divided into two separate loads to fit in the spinner. A minor inconvenience compared to the old mangle, now rusting in the back yard.

Finally, it was the turn of John's shirts, socks and pants to struggle and drown in the murky beige sea, and time for her next challenge. She arranged four Jelly Babies on the lid of the washer and watched them trembling in their sugary overcoats. Far below, with each judder, water dribbled from the undercarriage of the ancient machine and puddled across the honeycomb-patterned lino. Swish-churn, swish-churn. There were so many ways to eat Jelly Babies, other than just biting off their heads. She hovered her face a few inches above the dusty little bodies, enjoying the soft, candy-floss scent of icing sugar, then gently licked the nearest one until its tummy turned green before sucking it into her mouth.

Another hexagon of lino succumbed to the soapy flood. It was like a slow game of Blockbusters – *'Can I have a P please, Bob?'* She stuffed a rolled-up newspaper under the fridge; if the water got that far she'd leave it for John to see. Maybe then he'd agree to buying another new-second-hand 'bargain'. She reached for the next sweet without looking and tasted the colour. Red? She took it out to check, then gave the machine a nudge and watched soapy water ripple towards yesterday's crossword.

With the final rinse and spin dealt with, Flora carried John's collection of muted mixed fibres out to the back yard where the sun was yet to shine. Given the time of year, it would be close to two o'clock before the grey concrete turned a few shades brighter. While pegging out the last of the eleven socks, she planned the rest of her day. Saving up things to think about helped to pass the time, made her feel busy. Next on the agenda: choosing lunch. As per John's instructions, she was supposed to be finishing up the jar of fish paste. She pictured him tucking into his sandwich of squashed, sweaty bread with fishy-scented fruit loaf for afters. More fool him. She couldn't remember the last time she'd eaten one of those lifeless grey rectangles.

John maintained that anything more than one filling per sandwich was an unnecessary extravagance. In a satisfying act of defiance, Flora always created her own sandwich with a minimum of three. Today she'd have cheese, salad cream and grated carrot. Nice and colourful. And instead of sitting at the kitchen table, she'd have it in front of *Judge Judy*, followed by a little something from the treat tin stowed behind the ironing board. A French Fancy perhaps, with *The Flying Doctors*. Having lunch to look forward to was an incentive to get on with the rest of the morning's chores; carpets and lino, according to John's rota.

After mopping the kitchen floor, skirting around the now soggy barricade in front of the fridge, she hurried upstairs to wipe down the bathroom lino. She would leave the stairs and landing for another week and make do with a speedy hoover around the visible areas of carpet in the rest of the house. Finally, she began to line up lunchtime ingredients. Why have an ordinary sandwich when, for just an extra slice of bread, you could have a toasted *club* sandwich? A top deck of grated carrot and salad cream sprinkled with salt and pepper, toast buttered on both sides and cheese down below. She was weighing up the merits of triangles versus squares when she heard the unmistakable sound of a key in the lock. The front door opening.

John.

Quick! Switch off the radio, hide the salad cream.

'Flora, love.'

'Eh?' He never called her 'love'. She prepared for the worst.

'Something wonderful's happened.' He plonked a bottle of Lambrusco down on the kitchen table, followed by a blue-and-white striped bag from the butcher. Chops, by the look of it. 'Have a guess.'

'I can't imagine—'

He pulled her towards him, planted a quick, dry peck on her cheek. 'As of now and for the rest of my life I'm to be a gentleman of leisure. Retired.'

While she half-listened to what he was saying, a shroud of despair was already creeping over her like a cold, wet floorcloth. Everything would have to stop. Dancing to the radio, the stash of Mills & Boon, daytime telly, Gail's Cafe where the girls were so friendly. 'But you've only just turned sixty-three. Surely you'll want another job, something to keep yourself occupied?' Even the Jelly Babies were at risk.

'Don't you understand? They're *paying* me not to work! They don't want me going to the competition; insurance is very cut-throat these days. And I can't start a new career, not at my age. So, from now on, I'll have the life of Riley.'

What about Riley's wife? Presumably she fried a couple of chops and drowned her sorrows in cheap fizzy wine.

❧

John said he'd taken to early retirement 'like a duck to water'. He especially enjoyed digging the allotment on a weekday, while everyone else was at work worrying about the Millennium Bug and the havoc it would wreak on the new computerised system. Flora's ability to adapt was far less gainly. The age gap of seventeen years had hardly been noticeable in the early years, but now it became a yawning chasm; still waiting for her life to begin, it felt as though she were lying in a coffin with John sitting on the lid.

The only benefit of a househusband was having a second pair of hands to carry the weekly groceries home on the bus.

Soon they developed a routine: John waited in the newsagent, reading *Gardeners' World* without having to pay for it, while Flora followed the shopping list unencumbered, skimming a few pennies off the housekeeping and wrapping them in a hankie for later.

On a day much like any other, after the usual Wednesday breakfast of a fried egg on toast, they caught the number twenty-three to Coventry South Retail Park, chosen for its convenient triangle of bus stop, bargain-priced groceries and free reading matter. They stepped off the bus into a light drizzle. As Flora was about to rummage in her bag for an umbrella, a coin glinting on the pavement caught her eye.

'Ah, finders keepers,' said John, swooping down to claim it.

'I saw it too,' she said.

'But you didn't pick it up, did you?'

'Shouldn't we give it back to whoever—'

'And who's that, exactly?' He gestured at the empty pavement ahead.

'Then we should share it, buy something for both of us.' As they approached the newsagent, she pointed at a pair of giant-sized crossed fingers. 'How about one of those?'

'What, a lottery ticket? I don't think so – gambling's a mug's game.'

'It isn't actually gambling because some of the money goes to charity.'

The discussion went on for some time, but Flora knew if she kept it up, he'd eventually see his way to spending someone else's money on a chance to win even more. She clinched the deal by agreeing he could choose the numbers.

'Alright then, one pound can't hurt, can it?'

John's numbers were random, not the birthdays or anniversary dates she would have picked. No matter, they were in with a chance, and for the rest of the week she daydreamed about winning the big prize. The usually silent mealtimes became more animated. In between snorts of ridicule at her hopes for a new three-piece suite, John let slip he would like to spend the jackpot on a geography field trip, and left a copy of *National Geographic* magazine featuring the Jurassic Coast on the coffee table.

By Saturday evening they were equally keen to watch the live draw on television. No matter that John insisted on holding the ticket; she had already memorised the numbers and written them on a slip of paper that she wrapped around her lucky four-leaf clover keyring.

Spooky music and a swirl of studio fog heralded Mystic Meg's arrival in a full-length, purple cloak. Flora crossed her fingers on both hands. The fog lifted to reveal a crystal ball.

'What a load of old codswallop,' said John.

As the music stopped, Meg made meaningful eye contact with the camera. And then she began.

'I see a house,' she said in a spooky voice, 'with a blue door.'

'Get on with it, you daft woman!' John shouted.

'Lucky numbers are one and seven.'

'Hang on,' gasped Flora, 'that's us; we've got one and seven!'

'. . . a lady with long hair,' Meg gazed into her crystal ball, 'brown in colour.'

'What a load of bunkum. Complete waste of time and money.'

'Well, it's not your money,' Flora murmured as Meg disappeared behind a velvet curtain.

The drum roll for the draw made her heart beat faster.

John was supposed to cross off the numbers but he wasn't ready when number seven was the first to be drawn, and he was still putting his reading glasses on when the next number was announced.

'That's us!' shrieked Flora.

When the final number was called, she jumped up and hugged John. She'd already checked the rules – three numbers were a win.

'Calm down,' he said, 'it's only a fixed prize of ten pounds.'

First thing the next morning he went to the corner shop to claim their winnings. Flora had suggested a takeaway. Finally, she might persuade him to try something different. Chinese. Even fish and chips would be nice.

'Why waste money when you can cook a perfectly good meal at home? No, we'll reinvest our original fund,' he said, putting a pound coin on the mantelpiece and pocketing the rest of the winnings.

And so they began a weekly routine, taking it in turns to pick numbers for a single ticket and then sitting together to watch the draw. Their hopes for a big win were occasionally fuelled by another ten-pound prize. On one memorable occasion, Flora's numbers won fifty pounds, after which John poured her a glass of leftover Christmas Baileys and opened a can of John Smith's for himself. At last, they had a shared interest.

Hitting the jackpot would put an end to dreary old Grove Road; number ninety-three was the only house in the entire street without double-glazing, or a patio in place of the old outdoor privy. Flora searched the property pages until she found the ultimate dream – an executive home on Miller's Reach Estate. She would have animal print soft furnishings, a marble bathroom suite and a luxury fitted kitchen. Going to London for a makeover, like a woman in a before-and-after magazine feature, would also be a must. While she was there, she'd have tea at the Ritz with Barry Manilow – but she kept that to herself.

John said if she wanted to waste her winnings on bricks and mortar when they already had an adequate house, it would have to come out of her half. His share would be spent on a global adventure. Geography was his passion, but apart from a long weekend in 1959 when he had joined an excursion to Hadrian's Wall, he had never travelled. Everything he knew about the world had been gleaned from books and his annual subscription to *National Geographic*. His share of the winnings was destined to bring those pages of colour photographs to life. He drew up a list: the island of Molokai, the Salinas Grandes of Argentina and New Zealand's Punakaiki Rocks were just the beginning.

John seemed to enjoy the list for its own sake. Keeping it folded inside his pocket diary, he carried it with him at all times, handy for adding snippets of information. On the evidence of geographically fascinating criteria, a new destination would be added.

'I'll show you one of the most amazing sights you'll ever see when we go to Belize,' he promised. He spoke with so much familiarity and confidence, an eavesdropper would have believed they were heading off the following week. Occasionally, Flora suggested they should redouble their efforts with another ticket if they were ever to see such 'geographically fascinating' places, let alone know the comforts of a Parker Knoll in Maple Blush, but John was resolute.

'No need to go spending something we haven't got.'

'But that original pound wasn't ours and we won with that so—'

'Exactly, so we're ahead of the game.'

In the six years that followed, Flora encouraged John to embellish his list with extensive research. By arming him with a packed lunch, he'd go to Coventry's central reference library with a list of diverse questions – visa requirements, the national living wage, local delicacies – she could keep him out of the house for the best part of a day. John's fully informed world tour grew into the retirement hobby they both needed.

~◦◦◦~

'I'm off to the allotment.' John buttoned his jacket and checked for his bus pass. 'I'll sort out those spring greens and be back at six.'

Take as long as you like, thought Flora. It was always a welcome sight, him putting his coat on and leaving the house. She watched the front door close, waited to hear the gate clang shut, then filled the kettle and turned on the radio. Contact with the real world was music to her ears.

It had been years since she had referred to John's old school exercise book; she knew the housework timetable by heart and could cook the meal plan without needing to weigh or measure. Very occasionally the menu had been amended, but only when the cost of ingredients went up or there was a shortage of something. She had fond memories of the 1988 salmonella scare – with eggs off the menu she was able to come up with several 'emergency' dishes. But once the crisis was over it was back to John's boring routine. 'So we know where we are,' he'd said.

As it was Thursday, Flora quickly prepared the batter for toad-in-the-hole and fried the sausages to a pale golden brown, then emptied a tin of rice pudding into a saucepan for afters. With the basics done, she could settle down to a nice cup of tea and do the quick crossword in the free newspaper. At a quarter past five, she popped a heatproof dish in the oven with a dollop of lard. The trick with toad-in-the-hole was to pour the batter into boiling oil so that it began cooking from the get-go.

The next part of the afternoon's routine depended on where John was. Since he had gone to his allotment, she could catch up with *Home and Away*. Otherwise, if he was somewhere nearby, she would have had to stay in the kitchen and carry on with the crossword – it really wasn't worth being caught 'polluting the airways with inane chitter-chatter'. With the remote control in hand, perched on the edge of the sofa where she could keep an eye on the front gate, she tuned in to watch a heated altercation between Sally and Shauna. Other people's domestic disharmony often cheered her up. It was also reassuring to know that even in the eternal sunshine of Summer Bay, where parakeets were as common as sparrows and barbecues were an everyday occasion, people still had problems.

She gradually relaxed into a soapy haze, enjoying the nuances of yet another petty scandal in Sally's unfortunate life. The front gate clanging shut alerted her to John's return. In a well-practised move, she zapped the remote and hurried through to the kitchen. Instantly, she knew something was wrong; the customary warm, soft smell of baking sausage and batter was missing. She opened the oven door to see what looked like albino moles peering out of gluey, lukewarm batter.

'What are you playing at, woman? It's almost six o'clock.' John was washing his hands at the sink.

'It's not me. It's the oven. It's on the blink again.'

'You'd best fetch my toolbox.'

John had repaired virtually every appliance in the house. Some of them, like the vacuum cleaner, had been practically rebuilt, which thwarted Flora's dream of ever having a Dyson. The cooker had been second-hand from Buy and Sell in the local paper several years ago. The fact it had only cost ten pounds was a source of pride to John. He loved a bargain.

Flora returned with the toolbox just as he was spreading newspaper on the kitchen floor – something he did for virtually all repairs.

'Now, get out of my way while I sort this out.'

'Shall we have fish and chips? I could get some while you—'

'And let this perfectly good dinner go to waste? Over my dead body.'

Flora knew better than to argue about the batter being unlikely to rise and crisp up, let alone the toad's chances. She would dish it up regardless and see how he liked being right all the time. She'd refuse to eat hers and then have a quick cheese sandwich later, when he wasn't looking.

She sat on the sofa, itching to put the television back on, but picked up her latest library book instead – *The Tumbleweed*, a gloriously bulky romance following the trials and tribulations of Jericho Blake, a swarthy, broken-hearted man who travelled the world selling household items door to door. Flora knew if he offered her clothes pegs or a feather duster she'd swoon on the spot.

Just as Jericho was rescuing a drowning puppy, she heard a loud clatter in the kitchen.

'You alright?' she called, with a finger marking her place on the page. She read the next paragraph while she waited for an answer.

'John?'

She reluctantly put the book down and went to investigate. John was stretched out on the floor, staring at the ceiling with a shocked expression.

'Whatever's the matter?' She dropped to her knees and shook him. No response. She leaned closer to check his breathing, then laid her head on his chest. Nothing.

She sat beside him on the lino for a while, not sure if she should dial 999. It wasn't an emergency now. The house was perfectly still. Until then she hadn't noticed how loudly the clock ticked on the mantelpiece in the front room. There was a strong smell of acrid smoke and something that looked like scorch marks around the cooker socket. The old screwdriver was still in his hand.

His glasses were askew, so she took them off and smoothed down his hair. A pointless demonstration of affection, John would have said. She took his bony hand in hers. It was still warm. Why wasn't she crying?

Later that evening, after the ambulance had left without the need for blue flashing lights, Flora remembered what John had said and put her coat on. Although she didn't fancy fish and chips anymore, she would have her own way, just for once.

Waking up on the sofa wasn't new to Flora; whenever John's snoring became too much, she would creep downstairs and watch a late film. Lying full-length under an old eiderdown with a cup of tea and a packet of Rich Tea was a secret time of night she cherished. In the morning, a stiff neck would be compensated for by John's almost apology when he'd blame the snoring on his excessive nasal tissue and offer to take the eiderdown back upstairs.

A stiff neck was normal, but the thudding rhythm in her head was a new experience. Still lying down, she tentatively reached for a bottle of Baileys on the coffee table and held it up to the light. She shook it from side to side, trying to see how much was left through the thick brown glass. Empty. At least the Bristol Cream was still half-full. The crumpled remains of a packet of biscuits explained the sandy crumbs squashed into the carpet.

She vaguely recalled playing Jim Reeves and Val Doonican at full volume. John's entire record collection was strewn all over the floor; some discs were out of their sleeves. The static would be attracting carpet fluff. He would be furious. She propped herself up, momentarily confused; she still had her clothes on. Something was different.

No. Everything was different.

A pile of crumpled tissues. Bouts of wailing and blubbing. If only she didn't have a headache, she was sure she would feel better for letting off steam. There were more tears to come, she knew that. Thirty-five years of being Mrs Marshall had created quite a build-up.

FOREVER FABULOUS
SEQUEL IN THE FINDING FABULOUS SERIES
Coming Soon!

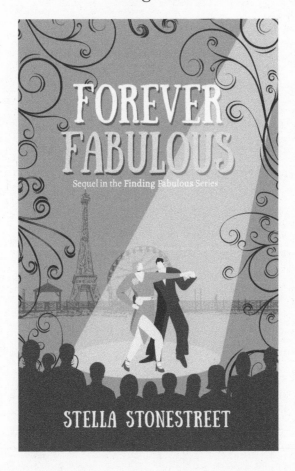